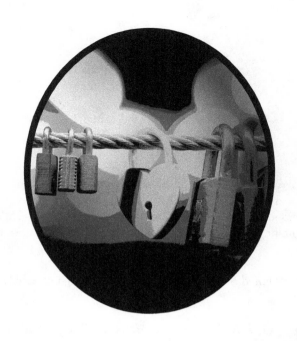

LOVE'S CURE

A TALE OF INCURABLE LOVE

ANTHONY LABRIOLA

ANAPHORA LITERARY PRESS

QUANAH, TEXAS

Anaphora Literary Press
1108 W 3rd Street
Quanah, TX 79252
https://anaphoraliterary.com

Book design by Anna Faktorovich, Ph.D.

Printed in the United States of America, United Kingdom and in Australia on acid-free paper.

Cover Image: "Love Padlocks on the Butchers' Bridge (Ljubljana)" by Petar Milošević (Wikipedia).

Published in 2021 by Anaphora Literary Press

Love's Cure: A Tale of Incurable Love
Anthony Labriola—1st edition.

Library of Congress Control Number: 2021913656

Library Cataloging Information
Labriola, Anthony, 1950-, author.
    Love's cure : A tale of incurable love / Anthony Labriola
    140 p. ; 9 in.
    ISBN 979-8-53123-855-9 (softcover : alk. paper)
    ISBN 978-1-68114-556-3 (hardcover : alk. paper)
    ISBN (Kindle e-book)
1. Fiction—Literary. 2. Fiction—Humorous—General.
3. Fiction—Historical—General.
PN3311-3503: Literature: Prose fiction.
C813.54: Canadian Fiction in English, 1945–1999.

DEDICATION

To my beloved family for their kindness and generosity,
and their promise that thankfully there is no *cure* for our love.

Was it to be laughter or tears—it came to the same thing in the end.
—From *More Pricks Than Kicks* by Samuel Beckett

PART ONE

Love's Remedy

I love nothing in the world so well as you. Is that not strange?
—From *Much Ado About Nothing* by William Shakespeare

1st Dose

Mamochka,¹ Papochka,² Heavenovsky and Me

What happened during a recent, trashy episode of the chaotically erotic and sadly ongoing work-in-progress of my life story was like something out of Gogol. No, I wasn't a rebellious nose, or a trivial tongue, or a fickle finger, or even a lone, tricky testicle that, as an upstart, had inexplicably attained consciousness, escaped, and was now living it up somewhere away from the rest of my abandoned body parts. My mamochka said that I was just an immature mouth. A mouth? Yes, I was a loud, lopsided, unflattering and foul mouth that babbled nothing but a feckless trickster's nonsense. Scorned and forsaken, as a consequence of my annoying, ill-formed and non-stop *absurdities*, I wasn't the sum total of my sloppy and bizarre body and inverted and perverted mind yet. I wasn't the human being that she wanted me to be. It puzzled her that my sub-human and freakish pieces didn't quite fit together.

When at last I turned 40, my birthday wish was that this birthday be my *last*. My fortieth birthday allowed me to be even more bitter and spiteful about life and love than all my thirty-nine birthdays before. I felt that I had been cured of any interest in the illness of life, and wanted a remedy for my sick obsession, not with a Gogolian overcoat, but with my uncovered (and therefore full-frontal) *love*. Still, the nude mood of bare-naked gloom pleased me above all in an acrimonious and virulent sort of way. Forty was old *enough*, more than I could bear any longer. As a former playwright and writer of children's books in early (premature) retirement, I, Anton Sergeevich Antonov, didn't want to live another day, let alone celebrate another birthday. What were these things called *life* and *love*, but unpleasant diseases, especially as I grew older? I agreed with Dostoyevsky in his *Notes from Underground* on the

---

1   Old-fashioned word for *Mommy* in Russian
2   Old-fashioned word for *Daddy* in Russian

question of aging: *it was bad manners to live beyond forty.* My sole pleasure now was found in the act of hating my life and its endless banality. I mourned the fact that it wasn't over yet. In complete disagreement with my mamochka, Zoya Ivanovna, who said I was just immature, I kept asking myself how and why, under the present circumstances, and, as a consequence of her lifelong siege of my freedom, I had lasted so long. And why? Why should I continue to put up with her assaults on my need to end it all and the maternal barrage of her infernal bullying? Was I supposed to live with smugness, triviality and bad taste? What the hell for? She kept telling me my feelings about life (and certainly my enmity towards my own mamochka) were unnatural. Everyone knew that I still referred to my parents as mamochka and papochka as if I were 4 years old and not 40, because that was how they had always made me feel, barely alive as with my mamochka, or decidedly deceased as with my papochka, it didn't really matter.

I seldom if ever spoke about my absent papochka, except to say that "death is not only the great leveler, but also the game-changer; death is the deal-breaker." My mamochka found these remarks odd and perverse. Did I miss my dead papochka? Did I love him? I would not say. That was for me to know and for my mamochka and the rest of the world to find out. At least, I wasn't a posthumous child. My papochka, Sergei Antonovich Antonov, was a professor in the Faculty of Mechanics and Mathematics at the State University. That is, before he died under mysterious circumstances when I was an adolescent. Though Mathematics, the Natural Sciences, Mechanics, and all Engineering Sciences rooted him to the world and anchored him to the universe, my papochka also had a fascination for language (just as I did and do): words, in particular, their meanings, origins, sounds and the rhythms they could (and can) make. He wrote poetry, as I discovered when I accidentally unearthed packets of papers tied with red string: *Poems and Other Mistakes* by S.A.A., with an epigram from the Latin poet Ovid, a reference to *Carmen et Error*, and what got that poet banished from Rome, and likely how my poetry-writing papochka felt himself an exile from home. I didn't like my papochka's poetry. One of his unedited, unexpurgated, unpublished poems (that particularly irked me, but I wasn't sure why) was entitled "Bone Box," in which the mathematician, trying his hand at poetry with images of the grave, attempts to tell the reader that a dead man's silence wins and settles all arguments about the meaning of life. His other major theme or literary preoccupation appeared to be words themselves—the power of the *word* and its significance to him as a secretive poet such as the following samples:

The Word for *Blood*

Words have no power to impress the mind without the exquisite horror of their reality.
—Edgar Allan Poe

Mud in his mouth,[3] carnage of crude words,
easy beauty, as he said, *of death*.
Dead words slipped into a torn shirt pocket—
suicide note, a bullet in the heart.
He passed by like slanting rain,
finished with words that were already

through with him, extinguished
tongue of fire.
A word for *chair* and straddling it,
like a motorcycle. A word for *unbent*.
A word for *unconstrained*.
Or, on the platform of the railway station,

a word for sucking in the coal dust
and piston steam that voiced
the solo passages of his spilled blood.
Each word, a stick of dynamite.
Each fuse, a liturgy. Only his voice stayed
behind, unable to speak the word for *blood*.

---

3   The subject of this poem is the poet, Mayakovsky, who left a suicide note and shot himself in the heart.

Ask the Words What to Say

Give away all the words you own.
Let them be. Leave them alone.
Let them go back to when they were

guests of glossolalia. Listen to the sounds
of their breathing. Hear what they utter
when you ask them what to say.

Words for You

I'm asking for the word that is made up
of limitless letters of a lost alphabet.
What's the word that appears wordlessly,
like a Blood Moon? Am I heading for the word,

or veering away from its eclipsing syllable(s)?
Which verbs ache to be nouns, and which nouns
feel trapped in speechless, motionless bodies?
I'm asking for the living word, not its magic.

Does my mouth speak only to itself,
and not to a sounding ear or a spelling eye?
What if all there is to say is saying too much?
From all my words, is this *word* enough to say it?

Words Fail

Grant that words can't find the word for words,
that parts of speech can't name themselves,

even when they find their likes or their opposites.
But words must find us and must be on the lookout

for those of us wanting to be found.
When words fail, they fail to find us.

But they do not fail—words don't fail.
I didn't find these words—they found me.

Still, I felt compelled to read and reread Papochka's poems to the point that I committed some of the stanzas to memory, despite my best efforts not to do so. There were other poems of his that I was forced to memorize by simply reading them over night after night alone in my bed. That is to say, when my secret lover wasn't *secretly* lying next to me. It was a secret because he was also my secretary. My poetic papochka dedicated his *poems* to a young man identified only as "T.B., my lovely boy." His muse was in his late teens, several years older than I was. I also stumbled across a reference to him in an unfinished fragment, a piece of prose, not poetry, in one of my papochka's journals with the title, "A Fictional Autobiography as a Figure in M.C. Escher's 'Endless Stairs.'" In it, he called himself "a beautiful man." Not in his looks or his soul or even his sense of what constituted beauty, but rather in what he found inevitably *beautiful* in another man, T.B. Apparently, this kind of love was catching. He went on to discuss the violently political activities he had undertaken with his lover, during their days of anarchy, waiting to die by his own hand or a secret policeman's bullet. He said that during the *Upheaval*, as he called it, he had tried everything to get it over with, even a suicide pact with his "friend," a devoted insurgent. His beautiful young man, like a Cossack warrior in one of Gogol's tales, wanted them to blow themselves up in the capitol. Though Papochka couldn't go through with it, his lover carried the reminder of it (shrapnel) on his right temple for the rest of his days. Papochka envied his determination to finish what they had started. They had wanted to destroy the society that hated them, and people like them, so intent were they on the transformation of life, the new creation they longed for, like lost and violent souls. The fragment ended with a vow to take his own life: "Tonight, I'll jump down a flight of endless stairs." Was he a romantic?

A fanatic? An anarchist? A dissident? It was all so inconclusive. I needed to know. I needed to find out, especially with all my rage.

None of the poems (or prose fragments for that matter) were dedicated to either my mamochka or me. My mamochka was 56 years young, as she said, and feeling younger every day. Ageless, by contrast to her life-weary son, she was in love with life; that is, when she wasn't being tyrannical about how it should be lived. With reference to her husband's poetry, she insisted that the poems were nothing but meaningless word-play, alphabetical ravings, always speaking of escaping, fleeing, in flight away from love and obligation, going away, but never coming home; and that was what he did: he went away. He had jumped down a flight of stairs to his death. Whenever she talked about him now, she called him "the Quitter." She reserved judgment about me until I was prepared to reveal myself more fully and in the fullness of my maturity. Would that ever happen? Where were we? She thought we were somewhere between then and now. I thought we were somewhere between now and never. Was turning forty too late, even for a late bloomer? The answer was somewhere between yes and no.

Despite calling her my mamochka, a term of endearment used mostly in the 19th century, but insisted upon in my time, she was a high priestess in a secret order of Red Witches, or so I thought in my unshakable immaturity and my perpetual adolescence. I often said so, too, in the matter, but substituted the word *bitches* for witches when it suited my displeasure to do so. Lately, I had begun to use the words *manipulative bitch* concerning my doting mamochka. Was this a natural feeling for the woman who had given me life? I whispered my contempt and shouted it, too, for effect, depending on the scenes she would make. Whenever I spoke about her to officials and would-be biographers, I said that she was a sorceress of the Demonic Church, so secretive that nobody knew about its existence. She was known to perform secret marriages, civil and otherwise. Rumour had it that she was a government official in the region, an agent of the new state. This was not the time of Gogol, Dostoyevsky, or Chekhov, but rather the era of the Federation, following the collapse of the Old Regime. If the end-of-history spin were to be believed, new possibilities abounded in the matter of matrimony, despite previous bans, especially on prior forbidden forms of coupling/mating/marrying. In the West, they were performing same-sex marriages and granting same-sex divorces, too. In the Federation, they were just beginning new experiments with living together, or so it seemed to me. It was an unspoken wish of mine to carry on my own experimentation with love and sex, but I dared not speak their names. Maybe, one day it would all come gushing out: my true desire. But there wasn't much time left, if I managed to keep to my timetable for ending it all.

My mamochka had hired a certain Valentin Alexandrovich Heavenovsky to assist her with putting her sick, marital ideas into practice, and to try to get me to marry. The young man was 25 years old and an aspiring poet. What I found most repugnant about him, apart from his dripping looks, was that he was not only an aspiring (or was it *perspiring*?) poet, but also my new, *unwanted* secretary. I hated aspiration (and perspiration), especially regarding writers. Mamochka's real motive for hiring him had a great deal to do with a young woman named Nina Akmatovna Akhmodolina. She was 23 years old, a curable romantic, if I had my way, and an irrepressibly *happy* person. I was instructing her on my world-hating ways, but she was a recalcitrant student. Nina Akmatovna was also my mamochka's personal secretary, and, in a twist that annoyed me to the point of spontaneous combustion, Valentin Alexandrovich Heavenovsky's ex-lover. They had had a whirlwind romance, but had abruptly broken off their botched affair. During the break-up, Nina Akmatovna had complained to my mamochka about it. Mamochka had tracked Heavenovsky down, and on the rebound, had brought him here. In fact, she had conspired to bring them together and work her black magic on renewing their relationship. Her goal was: matrimony, the union of one man and one woman.

Heavenovsky turned up on my blasted birthday. In close-up, he had a slapdash face, like the rest of his carelessly constructed body. I wanted to slap his face and dash off as he waved the paper in front of my nose and blithely recited a birthday greeting in doggerel from my mamochka:

> "*Happy birthday to my son,*
> *A very mouthy, Muscovite barbarian.*
> *Do you attribute your Ivan-the-Terrible-Complex*
> *To a forty-year-old birthday hex,*
> *Or simply giving up on sex?*"

When, instead of throwing him out right away, I drew him out with my special interrogation techniques, I soon learned that he was supposed to write *certain* suggestive verses that would induce me to marry. This was an erotic appeal that I found unappealing and unconvincing. If he had been Shakespeare writing me sonnets to that end (i.e., *From fairest creatures we desire increase*), I might have given it a try, or simply slapped his face, and then laughed my head off. Laughter was how I dealt with Heavenovsky's anti-erotic poetry. He was not the bard. He had invaded my private life and had tried to displace Taras, my personal secretary, and the only person in the world that I would ever consider marrying. But there was a ban preventing the banns. My mamochka had cunningly invited Heavenovsky's ex to come to my birthday party at the summerhouse: our dacha, that my mamochka said belonged to her, but that my papochka had actually left to me. More than a summer residence or a country dwelling, it was an imaginatively furnished prison. I couldn't escape all the crassness, inferiority and fakery that also ran riot in the interior. My papochka had given the place an ironic and silly name, "Shivorot-Navyvorot," as if it were an ancestral estate owned by a lunatic. In doing so, he meant "Inside-Out," "Topsy-Turvy," or my personal favourite, "Arsy-Versy."

That early, inside-out morning in midsummer, just as the Federation had emerged from its past, Heavenovsky, failed poet and unwanted secretary, entered my secret world with a gift for my birthday. Locked in my bedroom, I could see him on the monitor and close-circuit screen. In fact, thanks to my prying mamochka, a real nosey and snoopy eavesdropper, the whole dacha was bugged and under surveillance. This time, I did the monitoring.

Heavenovsky immediately set the box down on an ornate table next to a longhaired, stuffed cat. Then he took out a small book of *poems* (?) from his inside jacket pocket, ripped several out, and planted them strategically here and there throughout the vast room. Plants bloomed everywhere. It was as though the outside had been brought inside. Or better: that he was laying a trap for the unsuspecting "unmarried birthday boy" in a garden. He looked like a snake and slithered in a sweeping "S" formation through the dense indoor vegetation. He tried to deposit the *poems* (?) everywhere, so that I might easily find them. While eavesdropping, I heard the idiot saying that he had read about it in a book or remembered seeing it in a play in the capitol. He forgot the title, he said, and the author. One thing was certain: he was definitely not a higher order thinker. In all the time I was forced to know him, his quotient of stupidity remained constant.

"Possibly not native," he said. "But should have been."

He began writing furiously in his little school notebook, adding and crossing out lines, as if rerecording and erasing his every move, mood and thought. Then, as if singing an aria from a well-known, yet obscure opera, he said, "I love you, love you."

Hastily, he read it over, and then hid the plagiarized *poem* (?) in the foliage. He thought better of what he was reciting and whispered, "I love you, I love you, love you. Which *is* it? *Which* is it?"

Whichever it was, he looked as if he had forgotten it.

"For the time being," Heavenovsky said, "I attribute my forgetfulness to fatigue. I hate to use the word *deficiency*. When I haven't slept, I forget to remember, or can't remember what I wasn't supposed to forget. Then, on the point of forgetting forever, I suddenly remember."

He appeared to remember, like an actor in a silent film, and slapped his large forehead.

"Oh, I remember," he said in further deficit. "I love you, love, love you."

He remembered, and when he remembered, he remembered that he had been up all night, trying to forget his lost love. He looked around furtively and scribbled in his notebook as furiously as he could. It was as if he were expecting the ceiling to come crashing down on his oblong head, with me tumbling after, or the cats, turned feral, to attack him. The fact was that he looked as if he were desperately afraid that he'd be caught doing what he was doing. What was he doing? He scratched out everything that he had written thus far and moved cautiously towards the planted gift. From the way his hand darted back and forth (to touch or not to touch), he was dying to know what was in the box. The mysterious box, a gift no doubt for me, had arrived earlier that morning.

Head turning from side and side and nose up and down, Heavenovsky obsessed about the box and about his unfinished poems. Then scribbled something in his little notebook.

"Stealing from Pushkin isn't really stealing, is it?" he asked himself.

The question was a technical one. Was it a moral, rather than an aesthetic, matter?

"Pushkin is immortal, dammit," he darkly whispered. "He is in the public domain. Besides, from old books, it's borrowing, not stealing, am I right?"

Literary theft by any other name was *what*? He didn't know for certain, for (as I later learned) he was completely ignorant of all legal matters when it came to intellectual property. He paused, listened, and thought that he heard a cat meowing. He cocked an ear. Music played outside.

The musicians, most of them looking like old spies, KGB and secret police from a previous era, had been ordered to play all night long. You had to be careful, especially with the *entertainment*, because prying eyes could belong to accusatory eyewitnesses and lead to the kind of trouble that an arrest can make. There were those who were intent on knowing what my mamochka and her world-weary son (me) were up to. The authorities had kept a close watch on the place during the husband/papochka's time. You would not want these *musicians* as your enemies, not if you valued your life.

The so-called musicians, looking like thugs, poisoners, and troublemakers, played badly in a rigged-up gazebo on my mamochka's orders for the entire Midsummer Eve. They had obviously stayed the night and were now playing on, although slightly off-key. They'd likely stay on, then spend the day drinking and resting. They'd want a vodka breakfast. I hoped that they wouldn't eat all the strawberries and drink all the vodka. I really hoped they'd leave something for me to eat and drink, and then just leave. I needed a black coffee, a vodka shot, and a cigarette.

Heavenovsky went out and returned almost immediately with the strawberries and a bottle of vodka, as if he'd just remembered what he was supposed to do next.

"I don't think my new employer has had a goodnight sleep," he said to no one for no one else was there, and he didn't know that I was watching and listening. "I heard him shouting in his dreams something about music and damnation."

Yes, with all that tortured Rachmaninoff, I was on the rack. Darkly dreaming, I had been sleepwalking and smashing things in my sleep or waking dream.

Heavenovsky sat and copied out more *poems* (?). He wanted to go to bed. Yawning, he must try not to fall asleep on the job. If he did, my mamochka would put him out with the trash or banish him from the summerhouse.

"I want to shine," he said, "to appear before them, shining. 'Heavenovsky and his incurable needs,' my ex once said. 'Heavenovsky and his need to write, always brooding about nothing.' She also said that I was a sweet cheat, especially in the matter of love and commitment."

As if in the depths or the shallows of thinking, he asked himself why he was talking to himself about himself. No doubt, because it gave him the most pleasure, as in those notes from Fyodor's *underground*. He then called himself a *liar* and a *rat*. It was good to know oneself: he seemed to, in that regard. I couldn't have done better myself in attempting to describe him. Anyway, he appeared rattled and looked to his right. Voices came from upstairs: I made the noises for his benefit and to settle my nerves.

"Don't listen," he said, and looked to his left. "I'm not listening, not really; or at least, I'm desperately trying not to. I'm speaking just to hear myself speak and to keep myself from listening. I need company, and no more misery. Maybe my ex was right, though she never listened to me anyway. As far as I'm concerned, she never really listened, and never heard me out, especially on the subject of love. She never cared to listen to my ideas about making it as a poet. But that's not why I left her. The problem had been and still was that I couldn't stop talking and yearning. The more I talked, the more I yearned for something else, and something else was elsewhere. I couldn't and can't hear myself think that way."

He was reproaching himself for his neglect, ineptitude and procrastination: a modern-day Oblomov.

"I've written nothing new (or next to nothing) all night," Heavenovsky said. "I'm not ready. How did I ever get here, I who call myself a poet? Why am I on my knees before these people, begging a few crumbs of their good opinion?"

A few crumbs of their good opinion: I liked that.

"How could I ever have let myself fall so far?" he said. "Why have I sunk so low? The old saying is: 'May a duck kick you in the face.'"

I liked that too: the reference to a duck kicking Heavenovsky's face with a webbed foot.

"This *love thing* has got him all messed up," he said. "The thing called love, what is it, anyway?"

I had already answered that question, and could have told him, but he never asked me, at least not then.

"Between reminiscing about my first love and dreaming about the past," he said, "I simply can't concentrate. She was right about me. Why couldn't I see it? Why did I ever leave her? My Nina."

His Nina?

"Valentin Alexandrovich Heavenovsky, you can't write about the one thing you've lost."

Love? Her love? His love?

"Love blinded me," he said. "It blinds me to the way things were/are and the way they are/were supposed to be. All that I hope now is that I won't lose this job."

I would fire him on the spot for this intelligence.

"I have nowhere else to go and no one else to turn to."

It certainly would not be *me*.

Footsteps down a long, lonely corridor. Heavenovsky heard me, and quickly found a hiding place. He must hide and not spoil the surprise. What if I couldn't stand my new secretary as far as I could throw him? That was a foregone conclusion. As for me, I had fallen out of bed and had bumped my head. I was suffering now from a mild concussion. So could Heavenovsky possibly imagine what kind of crazed mood his new boss with a shock of Sergei-Eisenstein-like hair and a badly bandaged head was in that morning?

2ⁿᵈ Dose

Heavenovsky and Me

I entered like a Cossack. The room was crowded with my unseen enemies, especially the cats. So, with my cane (actually a swordstick), I struck at phantoms, but nearly missed Heavenovsky's back and legs. I wore a white bandage on my bruised forehead, like a victim in *War and Peace*. I immediately picked up my favourite book, *The Owl and the Pussycat*, from a stack of random texts on the floor. With contempt, I recited the words of Edward Lear, one of my favourite writers, as if with some hidden meaning that no child would (or should) understand, unless he were a little demon. I liked to read it aloud to unsettle my mamochka and her guests.

Heavenovsky, the hidden poet, popped up and burst out with a verse he had written for the occasion. He waved the paper in front of my face and blithely recited the birthday greeting.

"Who's that? Who's there? Mamochka, show yourself."

I raised my cane, like a weapon or a giant wing.

"Me," said Heavenovsky, nearly avoiding the thrust.

"Who? The devil, reciting doggerel?"

He missed my bloodthirsty tone. Thinking I was being willful or pretending to be hard of hearing, he shouted, "Not the devil, sir, but Valentin Alexandrovich Heavenovsky, the poet, your new secretary."

"Since when? I hate poor poets. They should be thrashed for writing bad poetry."

Again, I cut the air in front of Heavenovsky's nose with the sharp swish of the cane (using it as a weapon). This time, I missed. I missed because the cowardly poet had ducked.

"This morning," Heavenovsky said from a crouching position, backing off, and using the poem to protect his head.

"What happened to Taras?"

I swooped down on the intruder.

"He was dismissed. I'm here in his place."

"Taras was irreplaceable."

"I have the papers to prove *that I work for you now.*"

The papers were immediately produced from his back pocket. He stood up and presented what looked like a contract written on Claire Fontaine letter paper. They were just as quickly thrashed and trashed by me, who snatched them right out of the poet's trembling hand. Heavenovsky received a rap on the knuckles for his pains.

"She's hired you, but killed off Taras," I said. "Did she bury him in the orchard? More has been lost than my secretary."

I was poking my thumb at the note.

"What's that you're waving under my nose?"

"Your mail."

"It stinks."

"It's scented, sir. *Greetings.*"

"What for? What's all this about, Heavenovsky?"

"For your birthday, sir. Greetings from your mamochka, Zoya Ivanovna."

I instantly ducked. Horrified, I flinched as if waiting for the witch, Baba Yaga, in an unsympathetic mood, to descend on me.

"Get out of here. Get out."

From upstairs, my mamochka's voice interrupted the two-hander I'd created of our little, farcical conflict and contretemps.

3rd Dose

Mamochka, Heavenovsky and Me

We could hear what sounded like the beating of enormous wings. My mamochka swooped down, like a majestic bird of prey, making an entrance among jackals and hyenas. (This was my impression of her flight, descent, and attack.)

"Good morning, son," she said in her darkly elemental voice.

Sticking my bandaged head in a book, I refused to answer. There was nothing good about the morning.

"Aren't you forgetting something?" she said.

"If you're waiting for me to kiss you," I said, "you'll be waiting till doomsday."

"Is that what you social satirists call humour?"

"Ridicule? Irony? Sarcasm? Are they funny, especially when they are all forms of criticism? But I'm retired from that word play now."

"Don't make me laugh," she said.

"I can't," I said, "and the point is I don't want to anymore."

"What point?"

"The point of using dark humour to turn your eyes inward so that you see what's on the inside and laugh hysterically at it," I whispered.

Then I stared deeply into her bottomless eyes.

"Why are you staring at me like that?"

"I told you: to try to turn your eyes inward to your very *soul*."

My mamochka postured up and outfaced me.

"What do you want me to see?"

"The darkness," I said.

She pulled me closer, nose to nose, and said, "But what do you see in me?"

"Let go."

"What do you see?"

"Nothing."

She held me closer.

"Look closer. What do you see now?"

I was nearly cross-eyed.

"Myself in reflection, *cross-eyed*."

She let me go. Heavenovsky was still brooding on some of my earlier remarks. He couldn't figure out if I had used overstatement, understatement, juxtaposition or parody. Exposing his confusion and hollowness had been my aim. His lack of talent was my target.

"Now, what was I saying?" my mamochka asked, searching for words to say something.

"Were you talking to me?" (I had the words, but wouldn't lend her any.)

"You're a constant disappointment to me," she said. "Where are you going?"

"Back to bed."

She nodded at Heavenovsky who quickly prevented me from going (he was stronger than he appeared) by picking me up and putting me back into my seat, all at my mamochka's insistence.

"Put me down, before I fall," I said, in a crash landing.

"I'm insulted," she said. "I'm losing my respect for you, Anton."

"That's careless of you, Mamochka."

"You two are just like my parents," Heavenovsky suggested.

"Do you have a 40-year-old papochka, terminally bored, who wishes he were never born? Not to mention a mamochka who is 56 years old and thinks she's going on 30?"

"No, I mean you can't show each other affection," Heavenovsky said. "It'd kill you to be kind to each other, especially on special days. Why, at *home*."

My mamochka interjected before he could embarrass himself any further. She knew that I was likely setting a trap for the poet, and wanted to spring it before it was sprung. Snap.

"We're not interested in your domestic life," she said. "You're here to do your job. Have you written anything today on the subject I specified?"

"Yes," Heavenovsky said, "I stayed up late, writing."

"Well, let's have it," Mamochka demanded.

Heavenovsky began nervously quoting Shakespeare from a large collected works, sitting on the table. Following the recitation, he deposited the book and went back to his place standing in front of my mamochka.

"But don't you recognize it?" I asked.

"What? His love poetry?"

"Shakespeare's sonnet," I said. "This man is a *thief* and *knows it*."

"Is this true?" she asked, and continued to moan during his defense.

Heavenovsky was justifying himself hopelessly. "Yes, I feel so ashamed," he said. "It was supposed to be Pushkin, but I panicked at the last moment. I didn't think you'd notice. I couldn't think of anything to say about marriage. I haven't had very much experience with relationships. My own engagement to a young girl ended in disaster. I stayed up 'til three o'clock stealing lines."

"Imagine losing your beauty sleep," I said, "waiting to give birth to a lousy poem, and then stealing one anyway."

"Hullo. Is anyone home? It's me."

4th Dose

Marriage Quartet

Nina Akmatovna entered, making a trio into a quartet. She was excessively pretty, lighthearted, very silly, and overemotional, as far as both my mamochka and I were concerned. At least, despite our differences, we had an opinion about her mawkishness in common.

"Who's that?" Heavenovsky asked.

"A pretty, young girl that gets away with everything because of her looks, Mamochka said."

"Say goodbye to silence, Heavenovsky," I said. "Say hello to silliness and other illnesses."

"Happy birthday," Nina said. She kissed me madly.

"Can't you make an entrance, Nina," I said, "without kissing everything in sight?"

"Look what I've brought. Flowers and something *else*." She was whispering. "A surprise."

"Plant them somewhere," my mamochka said.

"On Taras' grave," I said, "if you can find it, but then again you know where it is."

"Who's this?" she asked, noticing Heavenovsky. "It's *you, Valentin Alexandrovich*."

She recognized him at once and tried to conceal the fact.

"What's wrong, Nina Akmatovna?" I asked. "Have you run out of things to say?"

"Introduce yourself, idiot."

"Which idiot do you mean, Mamochka?"

"Well, she already knows *you*. The other idiot."

"I'm the other idiot," Heavenovsky said timidly. "It's you. It's you."

He recognized her at once and tried awkwardly to conceal the fact.

"Look," she said, trying to be evasive. "Look what else I've brought."

"What, what the hell have you brought? I hate surprises."

Heavenovsky, despite himself, and missing the point, began talking about nothing. Nina, in his face, viciously, responded, and told him to shut up. Then to me, she said,

"It's your birthday surprise. A cake."

"That's the loveliest cake I've ever seen," Heavenovsky said.

"I didn't think you liked cake," Nina said.

"I can see you're going to be a disappointment to me, too," my mamochka said.

"I can't help admiring Nina's cake," the poet said.

"You're so very sweet when you want to be."

Heavenovsky, in an aside to his ex, said, "It's me. Perhaps, later we *could*."

"There's no *later*," she responded significantly. "There's only *before*. You missed your chance." Then to me she said, "I'll put some music on, shall I? We can dance."

"I don't want to move any body parts with anything more recent than 1981."

"Dance with me," Nina said.

"Never," I said. "Here, Heavenovsky. Take her into your young, thieving arms."

"I'll dance with you," Heavenovsky said. "By the way, I've taken lessons *since*."

"Very well, just this once," she said.

They danced. Mamochka moved in on me and forced me to dance. The tension between us seemed to vanish quickly. We knew the game and its rules: we fought for appearance sake.

"Aren't they a nice couple?"

"Mamochka, you're incorrigible. You haven't lost your magic touch, I see, for interfering in other people's lives."

Mamochka, to the rhythm of the music, said,

"Nina Akmatovna came to see me about their botched affair. I listened in silence. She left brokenhearted, not knowing what to do, or where to turn. Naturally, when they ended their engagement, she wept *bit-ter-ly*."

"Bitter tears at the trivial bust-up?"

"They both got a piece of that. He ran off. She went on the rebound. Had him found. I tracked Heavenovsky down. Asked him to write those crazy verses. As he from Nina, so his muse from him. Therefore, here we are. It shouldn't take us long."

"What do you propose to do about it?"

"Bring Heavenovsky back to his vocation: *marriage*."

"How?"

"Let them think they've met again by chance."

"Nina, so good to see you again," Heavenovsky said from his corner of the room.

"Not too tight. We're not in love anymore."

"You don't hate me, do you? After our big bust-up, nothing's gone right."

"I've almost forgotten completely that I ever had a fiancé. Why, when you slammed the door in my face, in search of fortune and fame, I almost forgot what you looked like. And now, you turn up here."

"Nina," he said, "I look like this. Remember me?"

"Shush. They don't know we know each other."

"So, they really know each other, eh?" I asked from the other side of the room.

"They met somewhere," Mamochka said, "fell in love and were engaged. All in a whirlwind."

"Then the kiss-off, nerves, jitters, fear of commitment. Just as quickly, he left her helpless."

"You mustn't hate me," Heavenovsky said.

"I've forgotten all about you," she said, "just as you wanted me to."

"How are they getting on?" Mamochka asked.

"They're dancing very close," I said.

"Good," she said. "In and out of love once a day."

"Still, she'll end up slapping his face. It's a face you'd love to slap."

"Seeing you again," Heavenovsky said. "I know I was wrong to end our affair."

"Affair," Nina Akmatovna said. "It was a shambles. When you left me, I looked for you everywhere. But you weren't there. I even took comfort in the arms of other men. They just wouldn't do. I had worked for dear Zoya Ivanovna before. When I came here, soaked in my tears, she took me in and saved me from despair. I was doing all right until I saw you. Now, I'm all mixed up. It's your fault again."

She slapped his asymmetrical face. It was a slap in the face of bad poets. Good for you, Nina.

"There, she's done it, Mamochka," I said. Then to the young couple, I added, "What's going on over there?"

"Nothing," Heavenovsky said. "Nina and I were just getting acquainted. But it seems she doesn't like my face."

"I don't like it either," I said. "I've wanted to slap it from the first time I saw it. Pour us some Vodka, and don't forget the caviar. A real homegrown breakfast."

"What a strange couple," Heavenovsky said to Nina. "Do you know why she hired me? She hired me to get him to marry by writing certain erotic verses, but he doesn't want to."

Nina fussed with the cake. "He's not the only one," she said and continued to count candles.

"Give this to Mr. Heavenovsky," Mamochka said as she poured the contents of a vial into a glass and handed him the vodka. "I prepared it myself."

"A love potion, Mamochka? Are they worthy of it?"

"No, just two, stupid young lovers, falling in and out of love. This minute, they're in, the next minute, out. But they're in thrall to me."

"Still, I'm glad you got this job," Nina was saying.

"Are you, Nina?" Heavenovsky asked. "Glad, I mean?" He quickly took the glass he was handed and swilled it down. "Can it be you still love me?" he asked, with tiny, perfect burps.

"You're very charming, Heavenovsky," Nina said. "Are you a little intoxicated?"

"Only with you, my love, and me: just Heavenovsky and Nina."

"Shush. They can hear you."

"Of course, they can't."

"Listen to them," Mamochka said. "It's going like clockwork."

"They're falling in love again," I said, "just as you planned."

Heavenovsky helped himself to the vodka and chanted, "How about a kiss, Nina?"

They kissed, while lighting the candles.

"How old is he?"

She kissed him many times.

"We'll never light them," he said.

He puckered his lips and closed his eyes.

"Give me deep and hard kiss, Nina," he said.

"You're drunk, Heavenovsky."

"I know. And you're beautiful."

He started crying.

"What's wrong?"

"I'm crying, Nina."

"I can see that. Why?"

"It's a birthday. You're here. I haven't slept all night. I've been plagiarizing Pushkin, and I'm feeling guilty for the past. I feel awful for what I put us through. It wasn't worthwhile to pursue poetry and leave you. I'm a fraud. And I'm so unhappy being unhappy."

"Bring in that damn cake, Nina," I said. "Let's get on with this birthday ordeal so everyone can clear out and I can go back to bed and continue dying."

"It's 11 o'clock in the morning," Nina said. "Time to stay up. What would you like to do on your birthday?"

"Take an overdose."

"What do you mean?"

"He means he wants to lie down *permanently*," Mamochka said.

Heavenovsky entered with the cake in both hands, and in his swaggering, said,

"What about the cake?"

"Put it down before it falls," Mamochka said.

Nina was steering him.

"Yes, do. Do, Valentin. Sit down, everybody."

"What does it look like I'm doing, stupid girl?"

Heavenovsky slid down with the cake and sat on the floor. Nina rescued the cake and placed it on the table. Heavenovsky let himself be helped up by Nina. He couldn't help it.

"I love you, Nina," he said. "There, I've said it. I love you. I can't stop saying it. I love you, Nina. Love you. Love you. Love you."

"What a poet," I said. "'I love you, Nina.' Steal every line you can, Heavenovsky. Nobody cares in this lifetime or the next."

"What's life without Nina?" He was weeping.

"What's that supposed to mean?" Mamochka asked. "Say something else, you fool."

"Don't trouble yourself, Mamochka," I said. "It's called *love*."

"Yes, it's love, real love, true love," Heavenovsky said.

"You're mocking me," Nina said.

Heavenovsky tripped and fell into her arms. Though Nina supported and propped him up for a short time, he soon slid back down.

"Have you got a match, Nina?" Heavenovsky asked in an attempt to help relight the candles.

"Poor Valentin Alexandrovich Heavenovsky," Nina said.

I laughed and laughed at my own laughter.

"You must find this awfully, awfully funny," Mamochka said.

"From my point of view, this is what's wrong with romance and your conception of love and marriage. What happens between a man and a woman, I mean. It's all very, very amusing. In the face of nature's tricks, when will they stop wanting to be freakishly happy?"

"You and your point of view," my mamochka said. "You'd destroy the basis of love with that attitude. Where would life be, if it depended on you?"

"Where is all this leading to, my love?" Nina said. "I should hate you."

"But you don't," Heavenovsky declared.

"Why don't you two make a match and get it over with," I said. "You deserve each other."

"You mean, get hitched?"

"Yes, damn you, it's up to you, and besides, it's one of the plot points."

"Am I ready for marriage?" Heavenovsky asked soulfully.

"A moment ago over there you were begging," Nina said.

"And now, he's sobering up," I said. "You see it wasn't love, Nina. It was something else."

"Not love? Something else? I do hate you, Valentin Alexandrovich Heavenovsky. Hate you. Hate you. I really hate you."

I was about to say: Bless you, or *gesundheit*, at what sounded like sneezing, but Nina rushed out, crying and sniveling.

"It's too late," she said.

"Nina," Mamochka called after her. "Stupid girl. I'll drag her back. I'll *drag* her back. And then we can have some more to drink, if the drunken poet has left us any."

"Then to bed," I said. "One good thing I won't have to blow out the goddamned candles. They're all over the floor."

"I'm so sorry," Heavenovsky said. "I'm so dizzy."

Supporting him, I twisted him into a chair. Since I couldn't cure him of his affliction, I plied him with more poison. That is to say, words that would do what my mamochka wanted him to do, and then clear out.

"I've fallen in love. But we were in love. We were engaged."

"I know."

"You do?"

"Of course. You two are types. Your kind shows up in our literature and appears on television. Everybody knows you're crazy about each other. But you're not sure about marriage. Am I right?"

"Naturally, every young *man*."

"Has thought about his hanging day? Are the arguments for marriage so unsound these days? Your worried that marriage is actually made in hell, eh, Heavenovsky?"

"Yes, and that desire, as the bard says, is *past reason hunted and no sooner had, past reason hated*."

"That's how lust works."

"Will she hate me once if we ever do get married?"

"Glad to see you thinking with your male repugnance for the married state, as we know it. There are so many alternatives."

I pointed at the mess he had made of my birthday cake, and he bent down to pick up the crumbs.

"I can't even persuade *you* to marry," he said, "let alone myself. What will your mamochka say?"

"Never mind my mamochka. She was never married herself, you know. Never *really* married. Has felt guilty about it for years. It doesn't change things, being married. For some people, it keeps things from changing. Nina, for instance, do you want to lose her?"

"To love and only Nina, and to be loved and only by Nina. But she hates poetry and poets. I'd never be happy with her."

"Maybe, it's just *bad* poetry that she dislikes. And besides, what's *happiness*? You'd be with her. You could have children. Pass on the Heavenovsky genes. Your offspring will look back to your marriage bed as ground zero. What am I saying?"

I was startled by the vision I myself had conjured up and immediately tried to put it out of my mind, or lose it.

"They'll grow up," Heavenovsky said. "They'll grow old."

"They'll go away," I said. "They'll go and bother other people. Then you'll be left together, husband and wife. Be as you always were: alone together, alive, barely, but still suffering from the sickness of love. And you'll grow old together and lose your hair, your teeth. You'll get cataracts, diabetes, high blood pressure, heart attacks, headaches, and backaches together."

"If divorce doesn't get us, or the *prenuptial agreement*, or the disagreements and allegations, or the betrayals."

"Yes, the divorce rate and the divorce court. It's difficult to love these days, to stay loved, and to stay married."

"Nina's the most beautiful woman I've ever seen, met, known, loved."

"To me, she's just a lovesick romantic with some potential in life and a penchant for kindness, especially towards life-hating people like me."

"Those kisses. They take your breath away. Those lips. Those eyes."

"Just think of it, Heavenovsky. She's upstairs, feeling unloved, unwanted. Would you deny her? Seize the moment, and she's yours. Wait a moment, and she's gone. In matters of love, your attitude should be one of gratitude, as my mamochka says, thankful for each other. Breathing together, as if in unison with the whistling of the wind and the chattering of birds singing her name. *Nina*. Sing it. *Neenah*."

"Nina. You're making fun of me."

"No, I'm letting myself feel a little sorry for you, truly sorry for your malady. You can't be cured of *love*."

"You're gloating. How did you manage to escape?"

"How do you know I did? Is anyone truly free from love? Can you ever truly escape from it, especially the love that dares not speak its name, filled with so much longing that you want to die?"

"Dare not? I see: as with Oscar Wilde in literary history."

Did I say that? I would hate to think that I was 'outed' as they say in the west by a bad poet and a poor excuse for a human being.

"In my case, I learned to mock it," I said. "Living has filled me with so much laughter, dark, as it may sometimes seem, cruel as it may appear. I may be disillusioned, but I'm free to do and say what I want, especially about love. Even to forget, if the pain of loving is too great. I don't want to call myself a man, a woman, or even a bird. The most important thing is to mock life, at least society."

"Is that what's important to you?" he wanted to know so badly that his eyes were crossed.

"Yes, important, unimportant, important, unimportant, whichever sounds better. *That* is important or unimportant to me, and my old secretary. Do you want to end up like me?"

"No. What should I do?"

"Marry her, Heavenovsky, today, now, on my birthday. And I hope it's my last one. To love and only her, to be loved and only by her."

"You're so clever. It all seems so inevitable. I suppose you're doing this to get rid of me."

"Yes, love's a force to be reckoned with. If you don't get love right, you'll end up in Siberia. You must move towards each other. Collide with one another and get into step together. The collision, the car crash, is called *sex*. Love is the sickness, especially for the lovesick like you. Cherish the simple fact that you were lost and then found by her. Love tells you that you're no longer lost. It tells you what you want and what you wanted all along. Well, what do you want, Heavenovsky? It's my turn to ask that stupid question."

"I want to pop the question."

Nina entered, as if on cue, dressed in an old-fashioned wedding gown. Mamochka held up the train. She was dressed as a high priestess of an ancient sect.

"Nina," Heavenovsky said in awe.

He was shattered by the vision of youthful beauty. Heavenovsky was on the point of fainting in the face of such beauty.

"Nina, you look beautiful."

"Just a little outfit I keep in the closet," Mamochka said. "Fits her perfectly."

"Lace, satin petticoats, mutton chop sleeves," I said.

"I was to wear it for your papochka once," Mamochka said. "He never wanted to see me in it. It's Nina's now."

"Your timing is impeccable," I said. "You're matchless."

"She's a perfect matchmaker," Nina said, "if only Valentin Alexandrovich Heavenovsky would have me."

"Would he?"

They kissed each other at least forty times. To sum up, they had met again and, through my mamochka's witchy ways and my enforced collaboration, had decided to marry on the spot. To my everlasting shame, I had aided in their incurable union, making myself sick in the process, and hoping to get rid of them in so doing. But they had decided to stay on for their honeymoon night. Of course, Mamochka had decided it for them. She was *mamochka-ing* them. She *mamochka-ed* all of us, my Mamochka. She was changing from a proper noun to an improper verb.

"I told you she is a sorceress, a witch, a priestess," I said. "I think she knows all about the dark ceremony and all the satanic marriage rituals."

"It took one, two, three, four people to get us to marry," Nina (the new bride) said. She was pointing.

"The marriage quartet," Heavenovsky said with sickening wit.

Mamochka, yes, dressed as an ancient priestess, as I said, presented them with rings made of white gold.

"'And they were married next day by the turkey who lived on the hill,'" I said, quoting my favourite children's book.

"For the sake of this company," Mamochka said, "to join this man and this woman in love."

"'And they danced by the light of the moon,'" I said. "'They danced by the light of the moon.'"

Wedding music marched in from the musicians, really police informants, thugs, stooges and goons, playing in the gazebo with the "I-Do's," and an off-key hint of "Happy Birthday." It was then that Mamochka handed me my birthday gift. From the gift-wrapped box, I plucked out a pair of silver rings.

"For the day you decide to pop the question," she said.

The bride and groom ran off to begin their honeymoon. That is, they ran upstairs to the designated bridal bedroom. It was enough to cure anybody of any interest in their kind of love, as if in an early, Chekhovian farce with jabs inoculating the audience against stupid marriage proposals and illusory, romantic love. In an aside that discomposed me, Mamochka said softly, wickedly: "Promise me, son. Promise me that you'll marry one day before death stops you from proposing, and that it will be sooner rather than later. Promise me."

She was harping on her old theme again: she wanted me to *get* married.

"Why must I promise? What a monomania you have, Mamochka, re: *marriage*. All right, I promise that one day I'll marry, if I *have* to."

"That's all I need to know," she said, knowing full well she needed to know much more than that.

"But what about broken promises?"

She wouldn't take no for an answer. I wouldn't take no for an answer. But what was the beautiful or ugly question, and when would we hear the word *yes*?

"Break promises, as you like," she said. "That's on your conscience, but don't break this one. Promise me."

I didn't know quite what I was promising, but I promised and promised, simply in order to get away from her and to look for Taras. When the time came to keep my promise, I knew my marriage-loving mamochka wouldn't like it.

PART TWO

I find the medicine worse than the malady.
—John Fletcher

1ˢᵗ Dose

A Remedy for Taras and Me

To try to keep my promise to my irrepressible mamochka, I broke out with this question:

"Where's Taras?"

That question was a difficult and damnable question. It was damnable and difficult because no one seemed to know where he was, or they just pretended not to know.

"Where the hell is he? More to the point: what have you done to Taras? Where have you buried the body?"

That was the *question* that I had been asking myself (but directed towards my omniscient though unresponsive mamochka) since last night. That is, shortly after Taras' disappearance. I had also interrogated others (mostly Mamochka and the newlyweds, Nina and Heavenovsky). The bride I disliked when she was there, but liked when she *wasn't*. The groom I despised on sight and even out of sight. *Hate* was a strong word. But I hated Heavenovsky, the new secretary, the one that had usurped Taras' job and had replaced him, but not in my heart. 'Loathe' was also a loathsome word, but the right one. I loathed him. As for contempt, it was best not to talk about it. But I had contempt for my doting mamochka, more than I loathed the bridegroom.

The question of Taras' whereabouts was an ugly one. It was an ugly question because it needed a beautiful answer. I wanted to find him. Had to. I longed to put a certain question to him that only Taras could answer. In a perverse way, it had something to do with keeping my promise to my mamochka, keeping a promise to her for the first time in my 40 years. It was a good day to do it. Besides, I wanted him. Needed him now more than ever. Yes, I had a certain question to put to him that *only* Taras should answer. It was that kind of question. The rub of it (together with Taras' disappearance and where to find him) had dislodged me from the needful comfort of my room to go outside.

Isolation and solitude were my needs. Still, I overcame my phobia and walked out to the gazebo. Walking outside was hateful to me: I felt too exposed. It made me spiteful, bitter. The fresh air did; the beautifully kept grounds infuriated and displeased me. The gazebo drove me mad. It was where the hired musicians had last seen Taras. Alive.

I had to overcome my inertia and lucid indifference to initiate the search for my missing secretary, the true one. Had he been murdered? Had my mamochka murdered Taras? She was capable of it. On a whim, just *because*. Hadn't she been murdering me ever since I was born? She had replaced Taras with Heavenovsky, a complete incompetent: a ruse, as it turned out, to marry him off to a girl of her choice. The absurd and sacrilegious marriage ceremony (an uncivil union, from my point of view) had taken place right under my own nose. It stank of cunning and maternal interference. She had done the honours much to her dishonour.

"Potato?"

That was the word that buzzed in my brain. I spoke it aloud and it buzzed in my ears. Why *potato*? *Bulba* was the beautiful answer to another ugly question. That was Taras' surname, or the nickname given to him. What else? *Bulba* means potato. Named for? Who else, but the legendary figure from a work by Gogol? The whole thing was Gogolesque.

Besides, Taras' head was shaped like a potato. It was unmistakable, on sight, and memorable, once seen. I remembered it, but I wanted to see it now. This moment. In the twilight by the gazebo, there seemed to be what looked like a large tuber, an oversized head-like potato, jutting out of the ground. Now that I looked at it in a certain light, aslant, it resembled a human head: mud-covered. Birds perched on it. One tugged an earthworm out of a flared nostril. Another pulled out another from the nostril clogged with dirt. Water and earth created *mud*, the fifth element. What was that line from mad Ezra Pound's poem about *mud*?

"Mud mired him down."

Yes, from the *Cantos*. Mud now mired my man down, interfered with his freedom. I called to the head. No reply. But then again, a mouthful of mud thwarts uttering any sound. His spluttering was guttural. With subterranean, volcanic spewing, he spat out his invective.

"Taras, Taras, it's you: you're alive, but barely. You're choking, flinging mud. You're using your dirty tongue to flick off those pesky birds. Good for you."

I recognized him at once, despite the mud, and even touched the muddy scar on his right temple, a reminder of an old shrapnel wound from his revolutionary, anarchistic days. Yes, it was Taras.

"Mud-kill," he said.

"Stop spitting and speak," I said. "Or rather, keep spitting until you can speak."

"Hand, hand, hand."

"Hand?"

"Ker, ker, hand."

"You're burbling. Hand? Ker? *Handkerchief?* Yes, to help you wipe that mud off."

I gave him a wipe: mouth, nose, and clogged ears. This was burial alive. Un-simulated. The perpetrators/gravediggers had wanted to bury him upright. He had wormed his way upward and out of his grave, squirming.

"What did you say?"

"I sighed."

"You said 'sigh.'"

"I said 'sigh' by way of sighing in the true sense of the word."

"So, you didn't sigh; you said the word, and narrated a sigh."

"I sighed, for sigh's sake."

For a man *gone*, or nearly gone, under the dirt, all night long, where being buried alive is the deal breaker in which death wields a fatal spade, he had a right to sigh or say *sigh* instead of really sighing.

All I could think to say was: "The cure for love, the affliction, un-simulated, like loveless sex in adult films as in American pornographic."

"What are you talking about? Buried alive," Taras blew up, or rather spluttered and splattered mud from his mouth.

"The pornography of violence," I said, "at the mere suggestion or hint of my tyrannical mamochka and her involvement in this despicable act. She is behind the crime against your humanity. She knows I have none, but will no one rid me of my mamochka? Will no one rid us of all mamochkas? We must invert our natural feelings to do so to rid ourselves of such oppressors." And I filled in the blank of what I meant, before going on with: "And the assassination, assault, mob rule, execution are *on. The gravediggers are not responsible. She is. She is. She is.*"

"There were eleven of them, murdering musicians, and the single shovel they handed me to dig my own grave, before planting me in the ground, potting me."

"Eleven?"

"The tentet plus the so-called conductor, Maestro Fartovich. I thought they were going to bang me."

"Bang? Bang you?"

"They hogtied me after they made me dig the hole, my upright grave. Then tied me up, planted me, potted me like a potato."

"Potato, yes, that's what I thought it was when I thought I saw it sticking up out of the ground, a large, head-shaped potato."

"Get me out. Get me out."

"You screamed, no doubt, begged for mercy to be unearthed. What had you done to deserve this, and so on?"

"No, now, now, now," he said, "get me out *now*."

"I see," I said. "You want me to free you with my bare hands, no shovel, no ropes or pulleys. Not used to labour of any kind, as you know, but I'll get those who can dig you up and get you out. To do what?"

"Kill."

"Revenge?"

"Murder the musicians."

"Why not turn things inside out, since everything is upside down? Stand everything on its head? Turn the tables, literally, on the world as they know it. Take the inside outside and the outside in. Instead of spilling blood, spill everything contained in jars, bottles, trashcans, canisters, and bags. Take the birdbath of the little girl holding a stone jar and place it in Mamochka's bathroom. Fill the dacha with dirt with everything taken outside. When taking the inside outside or the outside in, look for a trace, just in passing, of the place left bereft of even a hint of the explosion. Pass by without saying goodbye, or with nothing left to recall, nothing at all, or so little that the place won't remind itself of the lights or find a trace, let alone even a hint of the exploded sky. As seasons keep fluttering among tall pines, the outside sends everything away, and yet surprises itself each day. Come back only when changes are acceptable. Take the inside outside or the outside in, then rearrange the light waves when it's time to go, and never mind the one being left behind, or where you're going to, stepping into or out of the mess they made."

2nd Dose

Taras and Me, Continued

His command came in the form of a shout:

"Let me out."

I had to dig him up. I dug but failed to get him out.

"Everything alive will be below, and from below to above, everything will be alive. Taras, come forth."

Should we plan it? Or just do things that would avenge Taras?

"I'm at the Brr-ppoi."

"You're at the what?"

"Breaking point: Stage 2. At the boiling point, I must act."

"You must, if you're at the boiling point."

"The boiling point, the clutch: I'm at the *climax, conjunction, crisis, crossroads, crunch.*"

"*Last ditch*, I see."

"*Turning point. It's crunch time, Dunkirk.*"

"This emergency is making you spew."

"*Exigency, extremity, flash point, head, juncture, coming to a head, tinderbox, zero hour.*"

"Avenge yourself, Taras, with my ingenious help. We can plant them as pretty maids all in a row: potted musical flowers."

"Flowers? What flowers?"

"For the wedding ceremony."

"Whose? That poet and that twit?"

"They're married already on their honeymoon, so-called."

"Then whose?"

"*Ours.* Will you marry me, Taras?

"You're asking me to marry you now?"

"Yes, I promised one day I would marry; you'd be helping me keep my promise."

"You made a promise? I don't remember."

"I told my mamochka I would."

"Does she know the sex of the person you are asking? Does she know it is against the ban?"

"Must keep my promise."

"She is bound not to like the promise you are keeping."

"Promises are promises, like it or not," I said, showing him the rings.

"You've got to dig me up first, before I say yes or no."

"Say YES, and I'll start digging in earnest."

Under the circumstances (underground), marriage seemed the best option, certainly better than burial. He said *YES*. I dug. That is to say, since he had accepted the marriage proposal, I began to dig him out.

3rd Dose

Mamochka, Heavenovsky and Me

My mamochka was rolling her bloodshot eyeballs along the track of erratic, muddy footprints the full length of the hallway until she came to me. I was doing a handstand and walking upside down on my hands.

"What are you doing?"

"Standing on my head," I said, "like Father William in *Alice's Adventures in Wonderland*."

"Stand on your feet and tell me who has been tracking so much mud throughout the house?"

"Mud? Who? The dirty bridegroom is my guess. Mud? Did he make a pig of himself?"

I did a backflip and stood at attention.

"No, stop that, Anton Sergeevich. Was it *you*?"

"My indoor shoes, Mamochka, are clean: no mud on the soles."

"Your soul is filthy. And what are you doing with the little birdbath, my statuette from the garden?"

"Bringing it inside," I said.

"Put it back," she said. "Put it down before you break it."

I put it down and broke it.

A bridal scream from upstairs put us on high alert. I had given Taras (now unearthed) strict orders not to shower or bathe, but to get some rest. I had also ordered him to sleep in the bridal bed. When Taras had entered, the bridegroom was not there. He was elsewhere: the washroom, perhaps, a shower was running. Taras got into bed when the bride, back turned to him, spoke in anger about failure and defeat: that it had all gone wrong; and that this so-called honeymoon was a farce. Taras fell into a deep sleep to the sound of her bitter complaints about the bridegroom's inability to do his duty, or dirty work, as she put it. Fast asleep, Taras dreamed of potatoes in rich dark earth.

As if in a waking dream, the poor poet and broken bridegroom, Heavenovsky, rushed downstairs in his bride's white puffy slippers. They matched her short see-through negligee, which he also wore, unisex style. You see, she had hidden his clothes. Thrown him a negligee to cover or half-cover his embarrassing nakedness when he stepped out of the shower. He seemed to float down the stairs in a desperate need for comfort, solace, and marital advice from my mamochka. He certainly would not get any from me. I suspected him of being involved in the conspiracy to plant Taras.

"I found him (Taras) sleeping, befouling and soiling the sheets of my honeymoon bed."

In truth, he had been banished from that *bower of bliss.*

"It was you that soiled the sheets," I said, "that is, if you were up to the task, and, of course, your bride, if she were intact."

"That's just it," he said. "She said that the whole mess was my fault. My fault, imagine. I find a naked, dirty man lying next to her, and she insists it's my fault."

"You were obviously at cross-purposes in your crosstalk."

"Cross, yes."

"When did it all go wrong?"

"The honeymoon, she said. Now, she refuses to resume our honeying and making love."

"Please, you plagiarist, you're sickening me. I'm trying hard not to picture you doing that, at least, without laughing."

"Where is she?" Mamochka wanted to know.

"Still in the room with locked door and with him. She says she'd rather be with a muddy man, recently out of his grave, than a half-man like me."

"Half-man is good. What is the other half?"

"Well, she has a point. She always liked Taras before."

"Before what?"

"You came. That is, before he was buried alive on the orders of my diabolical mamochka."

"I did no such thing. Why would I want him buried?"

"To sneak this sneak into his place and position."

"What are you saying?"

"Buried."

"Why are you always so muddled?"

"What do you expect? You always insult me, and say that I'm

unclear in my thinking, that my actions, if you can call them actions, are nonsensical, and that I'm hopelessly childish. But are you a clear-thinking person with your social thought? Are your actions sane with the absurd role you play in in the farce written for you by those in charge? Are you really mature, Mamochka, with your infantile needs? Perhaps, we're the same."

"I thought you'd never realize the faint possibility that one of us is right and the other wrong."

"Or that one of us can't be right and the other can't be wrong."

"Which one?"

"No comment."

"I'll go upstairs at once to see about Nina," Mamochka was on the move. "Unlike you, she will do exactly as I say."

She stormed upstairs. I sized the poet up and down.

"Help me with this furniture," I said. "Take the other end."

I hefted a table. Heavenovsky did as he was told.

"Where to?"

"Just lift. I'll guide you."

Though it was heavy, we paraded outside with it and parked in on the lawn. I went back in with Heavenovsky in pursuit. His slippers were making it difficult for him to keep up. He slipped them off and hurled them into the pool. The next pieces to emerge from the summerhouse were chairs, potted plants, and a couch, even a sideboard, all arranged outside according to my instructions. I then sat on a high-backed chair and ordered the poet to haul more furniture outdoors. The interior was soon gutted. The rooms were emptied of possessions. They were placed in similar attitudes on the lawn. With a clock in his arms, Heavenovsky had to climb a ladder to put the clock on a low-lying roof. It was not the only item he had to carry up that ladder and to decorate the roof. It was an outdoor exhibit of what had once been a part of the décor.

He kept asked why, and I kept telling him to keep quiet and lift and carry the furniture. No mean feat for some of the heavy bookshelves and their contents. The negligee gave Heavenovsky trouble, what with the short hem that was riding as high as it was on his thighs.

I sat outdoors on a settee and drank vodka, while Heavenovsky dragged Mamochka's domestic goods and worldly possessions out onto the lawn, or up onto the terrace and roof. It looked like an estate sale.

It began to rain. I went back inside to an empty living room. The drenched poet continued to stand motionless in the pouring rain.

4th Dose

Heavenovsky's Solo

That was likely the cause of the chill he had caught. He was invited to come in and lie down (I invited him), but looking around, he saw only the floor to lie on. So he stood there shivering.

"Is this a honeymoon? 'I love you, I love you, love you.' And then this? Is it? Is this it?"

Whichever it was, he clung to himself, quivering and shivering and shaking off the raindrops that dripped down his face. For the time being, he attributed his quandary to fatigue. He hated to use the word *deficiency*. When he hadn't slept or failed to make love to Nina, he forgot to remember, or couldn't remember what he wasn't supposed to forget. Then, on the point of forgetting forever, he suddenly remembered.

"Oh, I remember," he said. "I love you, love, love you comes first, but not after. I have read it before. Pushkin? Shakespeare? Dostoyevsky? Gogol? Bely? Where have I read it before? *The course of true love,* and so on? I feel, I feel, no, I don't feel anything, hearing my own voice in an empty room, doomed to listen to myself when no one else will, or ever does. The incongruity, the giggling, I'm empty, numb, forced to speak out of my shame, and blaming myself again and again for my failure, not just with words but sex. When words fail (never mind), but when sex fails or I fail it, and I'm shivering from cold, wet, rained on, soaked to the skin, what can I do?

"Why don't I take off *this*? Oh, God, I'm wearing her negligee. Do I miss her already that much? Keep yourself from crying, Heavenovsky. Fight yourself quiet. No, no, I won't cry. I'm crying. My face must look as if I have cried all night long. I'm empty, forlorn, lovelorn, torn. Even my bad puns accuse me of failure. I'm nothing. Everyone yells at me. Why? They don't even know me. I'm tired. Why did I drag all that furniture out of the place? He was so cruel to order me around, and I simply obeyed him like a lackey, a flunkey, a frightened child. Why doesn't he like me and respect me? Why doesn't anyone like me? Nina? She should like me. She married me, didn't she? Did she do it because she hates me? Did she do it to straighten me out? 'I hate Valentin Alexandrovich Heavenovsky. I'll show him.' Marriage as revenge. Why? Should I kill myself? Would everyone be happier if I were gone? I became what others thought of me. Instead of avoiding it, I steered right for it.

"Now, I'm gangly. I'm dumb. I'm weird. That's what is said of me. They say I'm unlucky, too. What has luck to do with it? Luck? I met the right woman, married her after a false start, and with time and experience, I'll pleasure her properly, as she wants. I'll learn to give her pleasure. It has been so draining, stressful. I'm swamped. No, rained on. No, I'm buried alive (married alive). No, no, that's what Anton Sergeevich said: that he plucked that filthy Taras from his grave. The former secretary, too, is mad at me for taking his job from him. Not my fault. Zoya Ivanovna hired me. Is that her now? What's all the shouting and yelling about? No doubt, *me*. Anton Sergeevich and his mamochka deserve each other. Always colliding, forever on the attack, just like aggressive and vicious dogs. Of course, she has discovered his treachery, his moving everything outside. Perhaps, he is moving out altogether, and his anarchistic interior decorating is merely a stunt to make his vicious point/move. 'I'm getting the hell out, mamochka. Go to hell, mamochka dearest.' He is taking everything with him, like a vengeful lover. But does he have the right to do so? Does it all belong to him or to her? Is it the bequest of his dead papochka? Who knows? Who cares? She does, I think, or should. What have I to do with it? Nobody knows *me*. Understands me. Sympathizes with me. What do they know? It's easy to poke fun at me. Just look at me. But inside, I have a world. Everything is inside me: the books I love, the people I care about, my mamochka, my papochka, my sister and brother, and even Nina, are all inside me. Without them I'm nothing. No thing. Without them I do not exist. What else is inside? I can't remember: the sky, the trees, birds, animals, the weather, and history. I carry so much baggage, but it is my load, my life. Remember it, Heavenovsky."

He remembered, and when he remembered, he remembered that he had been up all night, trying to please his bride. He looked around furtively and searched for a notebook and pencil to scribble down his thoughts as furiously as he could. No pencil. No notebook. The room was stripped bare. The fact was that he was desperately afraid that he'd be caught doing what he was doing. What was he doing? He cocked an ear: more yelling outside, Mamochka's voice, my voice, and then Nina's. Was that Taras also shouting? Was he railing against the musicians, that gang of thugs, and band of secret police agents?

To recap, the musicians had been ordered to play all night long. They had played in a rigged-up gazebo on my mamochka's orders for the entire Midsummer Eve. They had obviously stayed the night and played on, although slightly off-key. They had likely spent the day drinking and resting, waiting and watching. They had wanted a vodka breakfast. Heavenovsky had hoped that they wouldn't eat all the strawberries and drink all the vodka. He had hoped they'd leave something for him to eat and drink. Was that when they had caught Taras, had stripped him, had abused him and had made him dig his own grave and had mercilessly buried him?

He was not sure but he thought he hungered for strawberries and thirsted for a bottle of vodka, as if he'd just remembered what he really wanted.

"I should be naked now and lying with Nina. This is our honeymoon. She is mine. Take charge, Heavenovsky. Take control of this situation. I don't want to miss her. I want to be with her. What should I do?"

He stripped off the wet flimsy clothes, stood naked and shivering. He would walk out into the midst of all that shouting. Nudity as a deal breaker was his form of protest. He would walk out to outface us all in the nude. He didn't think his new employers would even notice. He was invisible to them. But Nina would. Yes, she would notice how naked he was. He had heard us shouting as if in his dreams something about revenge and damnation. Without clothes on, he wanted to shine, to appear before us, shining. The recapitulation had led him to his moment of decision.

"Heavenovsky and his need to shine," his bride had once said. "Heavenovsky, and his naked need to do something to prove himself about nothing."

5th Dose

Heavenovsky, Taras, Mamochka and Me

N ina had also said that Heavenovsky was a failure, especially in the matter of sex. As in the depths of thinking, really the shallows, Heavenovsky asked himself why he was talking to himself about himself. Because it gave him the most pleasure as in those notes from Fyodor's underground, he called himself a failure. But Heavenovsky would become a protester. He would protest against our ill-treatment of him, all of us. He stepped towards the door, and stepped into the fray.

Before him stood another naked man: Taras. The basis of comparison was an invidious one, but at least Heavenovsky was clean, and Taras was caked in mud.

For my part, I was speaking just to hear myself speak and to keep myself from *looking* at the intruding poet. I couldn't take my eyes off Taras.

"You never ever really listen to me," Heavenovsky said, obviously addressing his weird comments to Nina, "and never hear me out, especially on the subject of my personal dignity. You don't even notice me. I'm invisible to you, appearing, if at all to disappear. You never care to listen to my ideas about life. You don't see me. I appear to disappear before your eyes. The problem has been and still is that I can't stop talking and yearning. The more I talk, the more I yearn for something else, and something else is elsewhere, even while trying to make love to Nina. Make love? It was a wrestling match with all those orders she kept giving me. How did she know about all those sexual positions? I couldn't think of a way of performing with all those directions, prompts and commands. I wasn't ready. How did I ever get here, in this situation? And no, I will not get dressed, and I won't shut up. Why am I always on my knees before you people, petty, contemptible, false, begging a few crumbs of your good opinion? How have I ever let myself slip so far into the mud? No disrespect intended, Taras, for all you have suffered at the hands of these wretched people. How have I sunk so low? The old saying is: 'May a duck kick you in the face.' It's a curse and describes how low I have to be to get kicked by a duck. This love thing has got me all messed up. The thing called love, what was it, anyway? Between reminiscing about my first love and dreaming about the past, I simply couldn't concentrate. You were right about me, Nina. Why couldn't I see it? You hate me. You married me because you can't stand me: to humiliate me, to show me how incomplete and incompetent I am. That's why I left you before. My Nina. My Nina Akmatovna Akhmodolina. Love? Your love? My love? Love blinded me; it blinded me to the way things are and the way they are supposed to be. All that I'd hoped was that I wouldn't lose this job. But it's Taras' job. It was a ploy. I'm naked before you in protest, nowhere else to go, and no one else to turn to."

Then the other naked man spoke. Taras spoke with words that broke my heart:

"Everything swarms. All things converge, collide, and then separate, part with or without sweet sorrow. Everyone comes together, hoping to stay, to settle in, be at home, in the desire to have found where you belong, are at peace, at rest after years of drifting or moving on or just forward, thinking one day you will find your place, be with the one you love or want to love, but then the swarming begins. Particles, pieces, and fragments from the dismantling lift off like fleas, gnats, insects, bugs, and dragonflies. They move in all six directions with the sound of whirring or mosquito sounds that won't end. All that stirring and buzzing of flies in the swarm of chaos. In such confusion is harm. Are there examples to anchor these floating words? Yes, I've worked here since I was sixteen years old and know from observation and experience who and what this family is and what type of swarming insects are attracted to their honey and poison. Even Antonov senior knew who and what you were: a cabal, critical of each other and the world. I heard the complaints, even exhausted after my underground ordeal. You believed that your vows such as they were would settle everything once and for all. But after the wedding ceremony comes the reckoning. Do you love, do you, or hate? You can't stand the one you're with. You can't bear to touch him or be touched. Everything swarms, and you must swat at it and kill what you once loved."

Nina flushed and gasped and protested that Heavenovsky was killing her and not the other way around. Expectation in marriage is one thing and mutual unhappiness is another, but incompetence in the sexual realm was unforgivable as far as the bride was concerned. No time to teach. No patience to wait. No interest. *That*, like love, had suddenly died. But was she cured?

Taras ignored her protest. He was more interested in Heavenovsky's theme of invisibility, and said the following:

"Despite appearances," he said, "appearance as *dis-appearance* allows deepest night to occur at first light, *dawn*. I'm certain Heavenovsky would understand this point well enough having lived it day after day, day for night and night for day. The sun, as our centre, doesn't have to shine, but does on everything new. I stand in it, as if caught, with only my body giving shade. Appearing to disappear this summer, impatient, hesitant, weak, faint, flooded with light."

"Yes, in a borrowed negligee," Heavenovsky said, standing next to the other naked man, "pink and white, then white and pink, avoiding, slowing things down, or speeding them up, insignificant, in successive changes, usual, unusual, even when buried alive, and always the same strange smile, as if knowing something others don't, speaking in the language of trees, darkly whispering of the falling leaves, about to get away in case you ask me for something I can't (and will never) give you, *this* for *that*. Anything you say about me (good or bad) is true, but truth has a double. In this altered state, when appearance as disappearance inflicts just enough punishment, I stand here, the invisible made visible, or the other way around."

"What do you think you are doing?" my mamochka said. "What is this absurdity you are spewing forth? It is some kind of farcical revenge, emptying out your brains with such nonsense and filth. Get dressed, the both of you."

"You can shower with Taras" Nina said.

"Ah, the fear of same-sex, is it, Nina? Your failure in the heterosexual world gives you the right to mock those who are of a different orientation and way?"

"And are you of a different orientation, Anton Sergeevich, a different way?"

"I could answer you myself, Mamochka, as if you didn't know, but I'll let Taras speak for me."

"Yes, yes, he is as he wishes to be, as he must be, and as he will continue to be of a different orientation and way," my Taras said.

"What way?" she asked. "He will suffer for it, especially here. This is not America, New York, San Francisco. This is elsewhere."

"We all know where here is, Mamochka, and what is in store. But I shall not be alone."

"No?"

"He won't be alone, I can assure you?"

"What are you up to? Oh, I see. This ex-secretary (covered in mud) will keep you company."

"He has accepted."

"Accepted? Accepted what?"

"I have accepted his proposal."

"I asked him to marry me," I said.

Heavenovsky was on the point of applauding, but was suddenly aware of his nudity and covered his puny genitals with cupped hands. He doubtlessly feared a *stirring*. As it turned out, he shouldn't have.

"I must get dressed," he said.

"You're invited to the wedding, Heavenovsky," I said magnanimously. "Wear whatever you like for the occasion."

"Is that what all this 'evacuation' has been about? A gesture? A piece of theatre? Treachery?"

"They are my belongings, Mamochka, as you know. I'm not moving out. You are. I give them to you."

"It has been pouring rain," she said. "Everything will be destroyed, drenched."

"They'll dry in the sunlight. I'm going to furnish the summerhouse the way Taras wants it furnished."

"I'd better bathe now to prepare," he said.

"Now? Is it to be now?" she asked.

"The sooner the better," I said. "You will do the honours, Mamochka, won't you?"

"It won't be legally binding," she said. "It will lead to trouble."

"Just say the words. Mumble them; jumble them, if you have to. No sincerity needed on your part. I'll take care of the rest. Oh, could you also ask the musicians you hired to come back for a second wedding party. I have a special request of them."

"Is that what you want?"

"Yes. Get them."

"I want something, too."

"What do you want?"

"Something."

"What is it?"

"More," she said.

"More what, Mamochka?"

"More psychological realism as in other families."

"No realism (psychological or otherwise) in ours or in this life story. Only Gogol will do and exaggeration. Long live farce and *hyperbole*. Let's reduce everything to absurdity."

"Do you think the authorities *will*?"

"Let me get away with it? What they don't *know*."

"Oh, they'll know."

"Will they? How will they find out?"

"I'll tell them. I'm compelled to."

"You can't lie: a pathological truth-teller. You'll inform; you'll rat us out."

"That's the way things are, and how it is," she said. "There's a ban on marriage between two men, a ban between two women. It will be voted on in referendum after referendum and will be shot down. It is not seen as a human right, even if that mattered. You can have the ceremony, kiss in front of your guests, take a limo ride and stop someplace for photos, but it is not acceptable, Anton Sergeevich. It is against the law. Live as you have always lived."

"In secret? Hidden in the open? Outside of the cultural norms? It is hypocrisy. Is it right for two people in love, and wanting to be together in marriage?"

"A *gay* marriage, as they're calling it in the West. Civil union, or whatever form it takes, is against the law."

"We'll work towards it, even from prison, if that's what it takes."

"Go elsewhere: where it is acceptable, or will be."

"Taras and I are staying here."

"In the meantime, what do we do with all the furniture you dumped on the lawn, the terrace and the roof?"

"Let it dry in the sun. Or have it removed. Give it away. Order new things—have them delivered as soon as possible. Taras will let you know what he would like."

"Why do you hate me so much?"

"I don't hate you, Mamochka," I said. "I'm *fond* of you. I enjoy the collision, our clashes, the sharpness of our exchanges, the skirmishes, as in *Hamlet*."

"You despise me," she said, "just as your papochka did. He had an excuse."

"What excuse?"

"He hated women. I had to take the brunt of it for his devious and perverse heart."

"What you mean is that he *preferred*."

"Men."

"Dear Papochka, all my life I have wanted to be like you, and now I realize that I'm exactly like you. But I do not hate women. Misogyny is not my game. Rather, I *prefer*."

"Men."

"One man only that has been the cure for what ails me years now and till death: Taras."

"Look, Anton Sergeevich, I don't want to be the one to disabuse you."

"Just abuse, eh, Mamochka? Disabuse me of what?"

"Your romantic affliction, your sick infatuation, all right, your love for Taras."

"Go on. Abuse, disabuse, as you will."

"But I would be negligent if I didn't tell you that Taras worked for your papochka as his factotum and toady, and, if the rumours are true, his catamite."

"He was just a boy around my age."

"Older than you, but just a boy, yes, boys and tobacco, or something like that from the literary or theatrical world."

"So, you mean Kit Marlowe, the English playwright, contemporary of W.S.?"

"So, is he sincere? Is he, as a lawyer and parasite, looking to continue his influence over your fortunes, your inheritance? He even had power of attorney of property until your papochka's untimely end. He controlled *everything*: the estate, the accounts. I had to fight him on your behalf, don't you see?"

"I trust him. He's honest. Has suffered. Should be rewarded. He cares for me. I care for him."

"Is this an epidemic?"

"Have I caught the virus of lovesickness?"

"So this is all in reference to *you and the disease you've caught*," my mamochka said.

"Of course, what did you expect? Am I immune? I retired from writing because of the burden of all the references to myself: my emotions, my perceptions, my aspirations, needs and wants, and always trying to turn them through stories into what others could read."

"You're not listening, Anton Sergeevich, you're not heeding what I say."

"Best not to talk about it."

"Am I prohibited from speaking to you about things that matter? Can I not speak to you anymore without your attacks?"

"It's the way of saying it," I said, "not to mention the horror that lurks behind your words."

"Horror?"

"It's the horrible behind your editorializing, the sanctimonious and self-righteous self-justification, and chronic assertion of your superiority over me, always knocking me down, trampling on me."

"I try to characterize things as they are."

"What things? How do you misrepresent my life, only to offer me a gag and a straight jacket that you want me to wear?"

"You are the one always using your rhetorical devices to escape making sense," she said. "I'm safe-guarding our values."

"Are you a guard dog, Mamochka, or an attack dog? Either way, you're frightening."

"Either way, I'm vicious, according to you, and so beware, my son, of the attack dog."

"*Suka sobaka*," I almost said, but bit my tongue for once, and muttered: "What a life story this is turning out to be. With or without a cure for love."

"Is it better or worse than my own?" she asked. "Or your papochka's now that his has ended?"

"At least, his is over," I said. "It's better that way."

"Don't speak against life, Anton Sergeevich, in this world or the next."

6ᵗʰ Dose

Mamochka's Solo

Imagine my hubris at the time in ascribing to my mamochka an inner life: that is, with a conscience and consciousness. Was I going too far? I had to admit that, for the sake of my tale, I had to invent such interiority in what was once called a soliloquy or monologue, as in the old plays, even an aside or a solo, because I couldn't claim to be able to read Mamochka's maze-like mind and get away with it. It was pure invention in defiance of verisimilitude in storytelling for the sake of going on with my story. At least, to limit my own omniscience, it was the pretense of letting her speak for herself.

"Let me begin a line of reasoning," she likely said to herself, "that will lead me to think this way about recent events: They are all lovers of the great reveal, all waiting for the miracle to happen, to love or be cured of the need to love and be loved, awaiting the denouement, the epiphany, the final revelation. They come to me to help them find their way only to rebel against me. I'm supposed to be the Mamochka-of-Them-All, except my own son, of course, who can't stand me. He assumes that he spawned himself with no mamochka for him, you see. And those so-called lovers, Heavenovsky and Nina, do they ever get love right? No. No. No. For them it is 'all or nothing': no accommodation, no compromise, no marriage of opposites, just poles apart. I realize that the great reveal in his life story is that there isn't one. No great reveal, no revelation, no running from the room, no shootout. Well, that is yet to be determined. No gun so far, but you never know. When will all the shooting start?"

(The last was inspired on my part as a projection of her thoughts, not really omniscience, despite it being my story. It was my intuition or perspicacity, maybe foreshadowing.)

"We'll have to wait for the gunplay," she continued, "guilty by association. As we found out last night and every night, a dead hand (the past) puts a rear naked choke on this moment and the next. Mortgaged to time, it chokes the life out of today. And tomorrow's tomorrow visits us in yesterday's borrowed terms. As I told Anton Sergeevich's papochka back when he was on this side of the grass: 'There comes a day for going, and in going, going away, knowing it will be forgotten, like a spell for coming out of darkness into daylight. And even so, people forget to get going and leave what they left behind on their way to find what comes after courting disaster, and that mess/massacre they left for others to clean up, like road kill. And who is meant to care about them, anyway?' Who will cure them of love? Me and the secret police?"

(Yes, *foreshadowing* for sure.)

7ᵗʰ Dose

Heavenovsky and Nina

The honeymoon couple cornered each other en route to separating, each wanting the last word before the getaway in the botched affair with the pangs of despised love after one of them had been dumped, and the other wanted reconciliation.

"What's wrong, Nina?"

"Everything."

"Tell me."

"I've told you too much already, all that I'm prepared to tell you too many times."

"Then listen to me."

"I've listened enough. I've heard too much."

"But have you really heard me ever? You say you have listened enough."

"Enough is enough. I'm not listening now or anymore."

"You never listened, and if you did, you never heard what I was saying."

"Your nonsense deafens me."

"All right, all right, do you remember anything I've ever said? What did we talk about when we first met? Or the day we walked home from the dance after the Lobov annual party? Or the vows we made by the lake when we went swimming naked in the moonlight?"

"We never did. You're making it up."

"We did, we did, Nina. I remember everything in detail, but you don't. You can't quote back a single conversation we had. You're an amnesiac when it comes to me. No history means we have nothing in common."

"I forget you even now. So go away and forget me. Would you stay married to someone who hates you and forgets you on a daily basis?"

"Sadly, I would, for love. That's my problem."

"Yours and mine. I can't stay with someone I can't stand."

"You are."

"I am?"

"My only love."

"You are."

"I am, but don't say it if you don't mean it."

"My only hate. I mean it."

"Then you married the only man."

"I did."

"That you can't stand."

"Now we understand each other."

"I don't understand a thing."

"At least, you understand that."

"It's just my luck that the person I love the most in this world doesn't love me."

"You're an unlucky man, Valentin Alexandrovich Heavenovsky."

"Unlucky? A big disappointment, am I? And you're lucky, I suppose? Well, I don't feel unlucky, despite the failure, the lack of roubles, the insecurity beyond it, in the money sense, to the core of my being. No, not even the crash on our wedding night. But I didn't stand a chance. I have been surrounded by unrelieved viciousness ever since I stepped out to make it in the world. A vicious circle surrounds me. It is so vicious that it has teeth to bite, to chew, to spit me out. It did not have to be that way. They could have helped me. Instead, they have delighted in hurting me, always wanting to straighten me out, to square me, to trip me up and show me my place. What a perverse pleasure they have taken in watching me fail and fall."

"Stop quoting others, just speak from the heart. I want a divorce."

"We just got married."

"Divorce, divorce, divorce. I thought you were worthy of me, but you're not?"

"Why not, Nina? Why am I not worthy of you?"

"Because, because you have to ask."

"Is that my true worth? Am I to second-guess myself as to how deserving I am to be with you? Must I worry about your opinion of me?"

"Not anymore?"

"Who is worthy of you?"

"No man, no woman either; perhaps, Taras, but he is unavailable for comment."

"Be reasonable."

"Don't talk to me in that tone of voice."

"What tone?"

"It's always about *you*, isn't it? Reasonable? What have you to do with reason? You're a ridiculous man or a poor excuse for one. I've told you how I feel. How I feel is the law in matters of love. It just didn't work out between us. Others think worse of you than I do. So consider it a kindness on my part."

"My critics? The reason you do not defend me or stand up for me against my critics is that you agree with them. You hand them a pistol, ammunition, and a blindfold for my execution. You're worse than they are because their critique is from the outside and yours is from within. It is the intimacy of your criticism that makes it so bitter, so spiteful and so shockingly hurtful."

"It is your obsessions that hurt others."

"We'll try again, Nina. I'll improve with practice."

"Practice with yourself, not with me."

"I love no one else in this world more than you: strange, but true. You'll miss me, Nina."

"All right, I'll miss you. When you are not around, I'll start to like you better."

"I love being with you. What happened to us?"

"I don't know: as soon as I was in bed with you, I couldn't stand you. Your strange body, angular, weird, those odd feet with long, ugly toes, your breath, those crooked teeth, and the list goes on."

"I have straight teeth."

"I couldn't stand you touching me. I *felt*."

"What? Nothing?"

"Violated, sullied."

"Sullied? You lay in bed with a truly filthy man, that Taras risen from his hole, and you say you felt sullied by me."

"Not physically. I don't know what the word is. I don't care enough to find it. Just please go away, Heavenovsky. Go away so that I can start to love you again."

"You love me when I'm not here."

"And I *don't* when you are. Get a lawyer. Get this thing quashed. Annulled, whatever. See Taras. He is a good lawyer. He'll do it for free, if you can't pay him. He is that kind of man."

"Is there anything he can't do?"

"Make a man out of you. It was so pathetic, you standing there in the nude."

"So was *he*."

"He couldn't help it: they had buried him alive. Besides, look at Taras and how well endowed he is, and just look at you standing there with your puny assets. *He* was wronged, while you thought you were St. Francis or some victim, protesting something that no one understood."

"I was wearing my heart on my sleeve."

"You had no sleeve, remember. You were wearing your heart on your private parts."

"Nina, you have gone too far."

"Not far enough. That is where I'm going: far enough away from you to adore you again."

"Never to see me again?"

"Never. If I do, I'll despise you more than I do now."

"Look, I was shy, awkward, slightly drunk. I'm off my game. Give me another chance, I'll show you what I can do. You can teach me to do whatever pleases you. Besides, something happened."

"What happened, besides disappointment and failure?"

"Best not to talk about it. It'll only get worse between us."

"It is the worse coming to the worst right now."

"Look, I love you completely. I love all of you: every part of you."

"You seem very interested in my nether parts, not my mind."

"Yes, you can never be too interested, especially on a honeymoon."

"But I'm not interested in yours at all."

"That's my loss."

"You're a loser."

"I'm a loser?"

"You lose at cards, you lose at poetry, and you lose at love."

"I'm a loser because you never let me win. Nobody does. Let me win for once, Nina."

"I don't know what you are talking about. I never do. I was not pleased with your lacklustre performance: no commitment, no sincerity, going through the motions, faking it. It was obvious (to me) that you did not love me, if you ever did, not in the way I wanted and still want."

"All right, if that's the way it is: last night, as you were preparing yourself in the bathroom, I waited, anxious, nervous, pacing around, poking my nose into things, your overnight bag, for instance, your belongings. I wanted to smell them and get to know them when suddenly I came across a little book."

"My diary."

"Your diary."

"You read it, you creep. How could you? You sneak, you snoop, you read my personal words to myself."

"I opened the book to see if I could find my *name* written there, with words of love, secret words of tenderness, affection."

"Vain, peeping, and did you find your stupid name?"

"Yes: the entry read: "I hate Valentin Alexandrovich Heavenovsky. I'll show him.""

"You're so mean."

"I'm mean? You say you hate me, and that you'll show me, and that I'm the mean one, and not you. What will you *show* me? Why do you want to straighten me out as if I've done something wrong? I'm deeply in love with you, yes, despite the mistakes I've made, and keep making, which I've lived to regret. Yes, I made a fool of myself with love, love, love all the time, and to read that you *hate me*, that I'm the only man you hate in the world hurt me. And what is it that you wanted to show me: to marry me only to leave me, to punish me for having once left you, to hurt me for loving you in my own way and not in the way you want?"

"Don't speak to me. I never want to see you again. Now, you've been shown: 'I hate you.'"

"But I want to kiss you, Nina. I want to kiss you."

"We've kissed enough, too much, and I still hate you."

"You've already said that, and written it in your diary. All right, all right, let's say I need straightening out, a correction, then correct me, straighten me out. Go ahead. I promise to behave. I'll keep my mouth shut and just listen."

"No, you won't. You'll do the opposite. You won't hear half of what I'm saying. You'll talk right through me, crush me with the weight of your absurd words. You won't let me talk."

"Talk. Go ahead and talk, Nina. I beg you. Speak. You can gag me if you want to. I'll gag myself, if it pleases you. Is it my big mouth, Nina?"

"You said it. I didn't."

"I'll shut my trap for you."

"Impossible: you are a compulsive talker. Hyper-elocution is your curse. Also, you plagiarize everybody, anyway, and never use your own words. Your ideas, such as they are, don't belong to you. They are the intellectual property of the writers you admire, mostly obscure, decadent writers. You live a borrowed life. Your thinking is *too.*"

"Literary?"

"Literal."

"Well, I admire certain writers, yes, and my world is literary. I'm made up entirely of words. I'm a repository of literature. Sometimes, I'm living in a farce or comedy by Anton Chekhov; other times, I'm living in a Dostoyevsky novel, *The Adolescent*, say; and still other times, it is a work by Andrei Bely, *Petersburg*, for instance. I admire them to the point of living them out. It confuses others, I'll admit. But that is my world. I'm yours, Nina. Why don't you want to belong to me? Why don't you want to own me?"

"Shut up, shut up. You don't make any sense. You want to own me is what you really mean, but I'm too dear for your possessing. We're simply not compatible. I see other couples having fun. You're just not fun to be with."

"Fun? Compatibility? I want you to be my lifelong muse, Nina. What have compatibility and fun to do with it? I want you to be completely *other*, in fact, the opposite of me. I'm not in love with myself, or anyone like myself. The point of the matter is that we don't talk unless I speak to you. We don't kiss or cuddle unless I initiate intimacy. It takes two for compatibility. You have no interest in any of my interests. I have to adore you, worship you, follow you like that trained lizard you had before you left home, the one that walked on water, you said, and spoke to you, just like it, and you get to whip me, criticize me, insist that I'm crazy and that everything is my fault."

"Everything is your fault. You're to blame."

"I'm lost. Why so much resentment? Why such hostility? Why do you have contempt for me? Why so many grievances? Were you always a collector of grievances? What are we talking about, anyway?"

"Straightening you out. Did we let one another down? Did we betray each other?"

"I don't feel let down. I don't feel betrayed. We may have disappointed one another."

"You failed me."

"That's *it*? That's all you have to say?"

"Bastard. What are you doing?"

"Don't worry. I feel a little dizzy."

"I'm not worried. I'm going."

He reached his arms out to her, spun around clockwise and then counterclockwise, for some inexplicable reason thought of Dostoyevsky, and fell face down on the floor.

"Insulted, humiliated," he groaned, "and incompatible," and then mercifully he blacked out.

8th Dose

Taras and Me

I attempted a compliment: "You clean up nicely, dear boy."

"Bathed and showered and bathed again," he said. "Someone will have to clean up my mess and the mess of my mess."

"Not to worry," I said. "I'll order Heavenovsky to do it."

"Are you keeping him as secretary?"

"I would fire him to reinstate you, but I've taken you on as my *fiancé*. They'll be other work for you to do. Besides, I think he has just been dumped, and to be fired on top of that would be the end-of-the-world for him."

"Yes, he has asked me to act as his lawyer in the divorce case."

"Another cure for love?"

"Who will cure us of our obsession, Anton Sergeevich? You know what we'll be facing: it is illegal."

"It is the right thing to do, my love. We can't cure it. The dis-ease is incurable."

"Before we embark on this illicit amorous adventure, I must be honest with you."

"Why start now, if you haven't?"

"In most things, yes, *but*."

"But, Taras?"

"But Taras is right. By the way, my name is not Taras. It's *Ilya*."

"Ilya? Not Bulba? Is it *mud*?"

"Close. It is a sort of *mud* or *swamp*. My name is not Taras, and certainly not Taras Bulba. That was your papochka's whimsical and Gogolian idea. It is Ilya: Ilya Vladimirovich Bolotonko, slinging mud and dirt, swamped, swampy."

"Gogolian, for sure, from Ukraine, just the same."

"Also."

"Yes, *Ilya*, what else don't I know about you?"

"In your papochka's time, I was a dissident, a radical, a revolutionary. In fact, I was in his *cell* in our subversive activity."

"Well, good for you and my dear, departed, radical papochka."

"We were *also*."

"Don't tell me, Ilya Vladimirovich. It's all in the past. Don't carry your baggage into our future."

"The past is all we have, Anton, and it never goes away. But I'll drop the load for your sake, provided you agree to flee from here as soon as possible."

"Flee, yes, we'll flee from here once you heal and feel better. We'll get the hell out of this false paradise, this living hell, and just disappear, you and me together. Flight? Agreed?"

"Agreed, but I don't really know what I'm agreeing to."

"We'll just *flee*."

PART THREE

He called unjust and deceitful everything that surpassed his understanding.
—From *Pale Fire* by Vladimir Nabokov

1st Dose

Nina's Solo

I couldn't be sure what anyone else was truly thinking, let alone Nina. But if she were thinking, and if her thoughts actually coalesced into words, and if those words had any meaning at all, they would likely go as follows:

"All I can think to say is that it started out with craziness and ended with it, too. The only male creature that I could trust was my pet lizard, *Iisus*. Men can't be trusted. They ride over you, or put you on a pedestal only to knock you down and crush you, and call you 'bitch' and worse.

"Gone, love is gone, dead and buried, and it was the difference between the fight to recall it and the flight to forget it all. Only a few degrees of separation existed between grievance and grief, mine and his. But one of us said, 'Who cares anyway?' He read my diary. And what was the point of knowing right off (the end, I mean, whether I loved him or hated him) or what couldn't be changed? He is a sneak, a snoop. Imagine reading my private thoughts. Only then did I know or take it on faith what I was once looking at and still looking for: myself, not him. Heard myself saying, 'Nina, I'm finally putting to rest what went on then, though nobody cares, despite the hurt, and putting to bed at long last the matter of what happened back there, which was an emotional massacre, beyond insanity.'

"Heavenovsky talks too much and makes me talk too much. We talk ourselves into corners and talk ourselves out of them, too. Talk, talk, and talk without end, and say nothing. We say we can't have kids because, well, just *because*. And we feel like fakes. And call on past mistakes. And wake up to find we're still faking it, saying: '*Authenticate us, authenticate us.*' So we talk ourselves into *authenticity*, and then soon talk ourselves out of it as well. No basis of comparison exists with any summer's day (or any wedding day) to the ones left behind with the pangs of despised love or pathways along false trails of loving and living; and don't make outmoded claims with no basis of comparison to the chains of those travelling with me on the whole long route to nowhere (once I left my papochka and mamochka's house), or that incomparable somewhere over there and elsewhere when I first met Heavenovsky; yet if you have to compare, even though it is best not to, then compare me to nothing at all, since no basis of comparison, usually better than the rest, is best of all. 'Yes,' I said to myself on the honeymoon when everything fell apart, 'no more referencing my life to that man, or any man.' That's when I got out of my head and into my right mind, and left. I had wanted to plunge into the future headfirst, but (and now I don't know why) I had wanted to take the plunge with him: yes, the loser, Valentin Alexandrovich Heavenovsky."

2ⁿᵈ Dose

The Other Idiot's Solo

Heavenovsky came to. Lying there as he was, he didn't want to get up. So he didn't. He just began talking right away. He would speak to the floor, if he had to (bugged with listening devices, the floor had ears) or he would talk to his own mouth:

"She hurts me for simply expressing myself in my own way with quotes and allusions, references to literature and art. I try to make everything interesting. She says she is not interested. Well, I'm interested. I'm interested in myself and in her. She calls me a failure, a flop. The point is not that I failed and that I fail, but that I faltered and I falter as each misstep sets me back. It is not so much that I fail, but how others succeed; and the more I lose, the more they win. For Nina, as for others, things get old fast in the matter of love. The disenchantments and lost illusions create a situation where *going* is getting away from what remains of the dead days. Or just how unaware we are of our losses when a longed-for and dreamed-of change doesn't take place. Things get old fast, and what thrills us links the speed of going someplace with getting old faster, refusing to last and sinking into the past.

"What entertains us is how easy it is to snub people or turn our backs on them and get rid of things, to ditch them. Before they get old, we just walk out, and, in walking out, hastily walk away. *Going* is in direct relation to getting away from loss and betrayal that stay that way; no delay in moving on, collecting fragments of a wasted past.

"With courage, we talk ourselves into anything. And in fear, we talk ourselves out of anything too. We can fast-talk ourselves into a corner. And just as fast, talk ourselves out of it, too. We say we can't sing, because we can't stand the sound of our own voices. And we say we can't dance at the party, because we keep tripping over our own feet. So we say we feel like fakes and call on past mistakes as evidence. Still faking it, we say: 'Not afraid anymore.' We talk ourselves into courage and hope. But soon, we talk ourselves out of them as well. In the face of insult and humiliation, we deny our deniers. Why do I do it? Why do I continue to do what I do? Why did I do anything I did in the past?

"Let things of the past stay in the past, even the shames that interlope, usurp, last and that will outlast us. Yesterday's dead have no right to claim today. Isn't it enough that there has been a loss? Why agonize over what it signifies? Over and done with, come and gone, a vicious circle, a complete act. So go on with the new day, Heavenovsky, another day, and live for one new thing. Call that tomorrow.' Tomorrow. Tomorrow. Tomorrow. I'm just talking to my own mouth or talking to the floor."

He was flat out. Then realized that a duck, if it were to come waddling by, could kick him with webbed feet in the face (that is to say, a duck or anyone of us waddling by, duck-like, could), and so, in defiance, and to prevent it, he stood up.

3rd Dose

Ilya and Me in the Inside Outside[4]

Preparing to flee from the false paradise of the summerhouse suited us just fine. He had to recover, to get better, before we could go. In the face of time passing in his wished-for healing (it seemed like day and night, and night for day, or the other way around, but it was likely just my concept of time), I kept saying over and over again:

"The wild boy went wilding out for bringing the outdoors in, the beautiful boy child became wild."

Was this what I was thinking of Ilya as I headed right for him? As part of his healing (he had been buried alive), he kept bringing the outside inside, plants, birds, tiny animals, chipmunks, squirrels, even a baby raccoon, tending to the indoor flora and fauna, and taking it back outside when Mamochka ordered Heavenovsky in a blunt way to remove them from the *inside,* which was really my place. Our lives were upside down. What else could either of us do?

"Help me with the squirrels, Anton," Ilya said, seeing me landing with my arms outstretched as if helicoptering on an airstrip.

"Do you really want to be indoors?" I asked, thinking how I had once taken the inside outside myself, but in a different sense.

"Sometimes, I think of switching the two," he said. "Sometimes I think they do switch, or would, if they only knew what was good for them, but sometimes, they want to be outside; the inside and outside have always been difficult to distinguish, well, for rats and raccoons, anyway. I'm going to give it more thought with squirrels, but the plants and trees I've brought in help to make it more 'natural' for them, don't you think, in the habitat sense?"

"All right, in that sense, it seems more natural."

---

4   Scene is very loosely based on a sequence in *Dragonfly's Urban Crusade.*

"This is how we should live, anyway. We should switch. We should stop rebelling against nature and the natural world, and let it reclaim us."

"Just the way dragonflies do," I said.

"Exactly," Ilya said. "They've been around since the beginning. I wish I was a damselfly."

"Fun facts about Dragonflies," I said, "in the Order of Odonata. Toothed ones, they have serrated teeth and eat meat, and all the mosquitoes you got; have four wings, and can fly like helicopters; can also live the life aquatic; a dragonfly's head is almost all eye; the ones known as *globe skimmers* can fly 11,000 miles and back in migration."

"I want to be a globe skimmer with you," he said in a sudden but natural flush. "Let's fly 11,000 miles and back, like twin dragonflies, return to the natural world and live like that."

Was he saying what he really meant? Did he mean what he said? I wanted nothing better than to helicopter with him one day away from here, and away from the pain of rebelling against nature. I knew now I loved him dearly, deeply, inevitably, wounded as he was, with the momentum of bringing the outside inside, to change the order of things, or reestablish the natural order.

But what did my new love for him and his "love of nature" have to do with the story I was working on?

"Well, here we are," Ilya said. "That's how it is, and how it is *is* what it is."

"Then there we are," I said.

"There is in people such vagueness," Ilya said, "that they can influence you in a positive or negative way, and both at the same time. That goes for prejudice as well."

"We're vague, you're right. Prejudice, yes, it is spiteful, hateful, and can destroy love."

"But it can be of use," he said, "especially when things begin, but not in love or war."

I wasn't sure how to take it, his view of vagueness, though I understood the theme of prejudice. I was thin-skinned and sensitive that way. If you cried, I cried. If you got sick, I got sick. An empathic hysteric, I guessed I was an *empathic hysteric*. But I liked to think of it as mirroring empathy, and complicated compassion. I had a feeling brain, or no brain at all, and liked no brainers. I could identify with everybody, every living thing, and even inanimate objects, but didn't always want to. People and things didn't like me, but I liked them: stones, dead leaves, hammers, nails, books, Ilya. I cared about them all, and felt what they felt, or what I felt they felt.

"Right," I said, remembering, and recalling, too, that as a writer (a kind of detective) looking for clues and clues of clues in other people's lives so that I could write about them and solve the mystery of their lives like a Sherlock Holmes detective mystery, and I could also use the secret weapon of words: yes, words that kill like a death ray, and a spew of deadly breath that can paralyze the prey, like a Basilisk.

"Say your prayers if I talk at you," I said, "talk into you, as it were, with deadly intent and mortal rhetoric. Look out if I *haw* on you with my fire-breathing dragon's breath, which will really feel like acid. It reminds my victims just before their demise of the Basilisk, if they know what that mythic creature is, or really was."

"King of the Serpents," Ilya said. "That's how nature is, killing with a breath or look, and we're all a part of the bestiary."

"I like that," I said, "the bit about nature and the bestiary. That's a good thing, especially if you are trying to escape."

"I'm trying to escape," Ilya whispered, potting a plant. "I thought you had a lethal thing for me," he whispered.

"*Had* is not having," I barely breathed. "Lethal is no longer where it's at where love is concerned."

"Where's it at?" he asked.

"Here," I said, touching the flower.

Still, what was the link between this moment and the story I was living through, the plot I was struggling to put together, and the weird themes that obsessed me? I figured that moving the outside inside and falling for Ilya had something essential and something ultimate to do with it, but I couldn't think of just what that was, not right now, because, right now, my writer's thoughts were cloud-formations drifting, drifting in a wide-open sky of incurable love and self-deception, and my judgment was like a dragonfly of the Order of Odonata living inside and feeling trapped in this place, and wanting to get the hell away.

"Do you ever get the feeling you've been had, are being had?" Ilya asked.

"Yes, bad," I said, "*but*."

"But what?"

"I let people and things have me, use me, manipulate and get the better of me, despite my prickliness."

"Why?"

"Because they feel they have to make a fool out of me, *and*."

"And what, my sweet Anton?"

"I want something else. I want to know the truth behind the deception, the real behind the real, so we're both content, used and using. I want you to understand."

"What?"

"To realize."

"To realize what?"

"That I."

"That you like me, and can learn to do more. I get it, especially if I swallow hard. But to me, in all this darkness, I see it differently."

"How do you see it? How do you understand it?"

"You're just another accomplice."

"No," I whispered, accepting a ladybug on my open palm from the tips of Ilya's beautiful fingers. "I'm on your side: I'm for you. I sympathize."

"By the way," Ilya said, now holding a bird, a yellow warbler, in the cage of his hands, "I used to write fantasy poems about you back in the day, living vicariously, a plagiarized life."

"It was *you*," I said, "not my papochka."

"It was *me*," he said, "not him. I liked you from the start. I did not want to plagiarize his kind of love. Mine is totally original: a just man seeking another just man, and not just a man. You are original, too. But do you get to save me?"

"You?"

"Me."

"That's got to be a good thing: something I must work on, develop as part of the story I'm living through, *especially*."

"Especially if we love each other."

4ᵗʰ Dose

Wordplay with Papochka's Ghost

Making preparations exhausted me. I usually did nothing. I talked, but despised working. I had a strange dream, or an hallucination, seeing things that night: my deceased Papochka appeared to me (like the Ghost to Hamlet) and said that he was *game* for anything.

"Are you sure you can do *this*?" I asked, "given that you no longer exist and that you are an apparition?"

"Are *you* sure *you* can do this, word boy," Papochka answered me by asking, "given your need to be cured of love?"

"I don't know if there is a cure. It's only wordplay: I get out my dictionary and find more words for better wordplay: puns and the like to delight and to dazzle, fitting words to thoughts and thoughts to sound effects. It is the force of words I'm after."

"You're temporarily gagged, get back to writing and speaking as soon as possible, even with a wounded writing hand and a hurt mouth," Papochka said, "until you can't write or speak anymore. You'll have to speak up soon enough."

"Are you really up to this?" I asked again, almost tenderly, "especially with the one that you abandoned as a child by taking your own life?"

"The best thing for it," Papochka said, "talking and philosophizing with you is a good thing, in my ghostly condition, especially with my son. But what about the way you're turning your back on storytelling? Aren't you afraid of paralysis?"

"Afraid?" I thought about it. "I'm not sure if *afraid* is the right word when I'm trying to finish the story that I've started, and not knowing how it will turn out, but I don't want to end up in a wheelchair. Then again, *paralysis,* I don't know. When I used to publish, I spent time recovering from nasty reviews. I felt broken-hearted and gagged. Thought I was finished. Took a year to recover. Smashed my brow against a wall, asking why, why, why, was I a failed writer, a neurotic? Reconstructed my stories, and after some stiffness in style, still tried something new, *so*."

"So you and Ilya are now in the same story?" my papochka's ghost asked.

"I'm in it with Ilya, to save him. And your part of the story is past, Papochka, the fiction that no one believes anymore."

"Not Ilya's?"

"Well, yes, now that I'm into it, I'm into it more for Ilya's sake than for anybody else's. Funny that."

"And what have I to do with any of this, besides having loved him myself? Jealousy? Are you jealous of the dead?"

"Not sure, and hoping you could tell me, *or*."

"Look, I never invent or make up a story and that's the truth of it. At least, *my* truth, and I find it beautiful. I never deceived your mamochka. I showed her how I felt about other women and men right in front of her. I gave her everything she wanted, but she wanted loyalty, submission, and she wanted to blame me for her jealousy and mental illness. I let her until it went too far."

"How far is too far?"

"*This* far."

"Where we are?"

"And here you are looking for God knows what exactly in this so-called dream? Is it the jitters before your wedding day?"

"I'm looking for evidence of compassion."

"You make me laugh. Compassion?"

"Empathy."

"Feelings? Am I right?"

"You're right there."

"About what?"

"Well, about the people you hurt for one thing."

"People I hurt loved to be hurt and hurt good and hurt often and hurt by me."

"Right, right."

"You write about your dreams. It's always castles in the air."

A quick scene change in the dream, and I glimpsed faces in the windows.

"Faces in the windows," Papochka's ghost said, "curious little eyes. Of course, they want to know if the dead come back to haunt you? Here I am. Do I haunt you? Hey, look: there's Mamochka in the window. Her stare is a death ray and can kill and can burn a hole right in your heart and groin, and destroy your soul. The *kids*, Nina, Ilya, Heavenovsky, are looking at us, too; so just smile up at them, and let them think we're getting along, you and your papochka's ghost. And now, at this time of my non-being, I still do the same as I did when I was alive."

"What do you do, Papochka, in that undiscovered country?"

"Long to live. So, Anton, live, and love, but one day, you'll have to get back to your vocation."

"My calling?"

"To writing, but to write, you must write. But first, congratulations."

"For what?"

"Your wedding day."

In the dream, the room opened up, as walls fell away, and we talked along walkways, down steps, held onto crooked railings, and continued the interrogation, confab, chat, or whatever it was, and interview in the same vein. Each speaker had his own verbal tricks or stunts to perform with language and with the questions and answers. I knew and didn't exactly know what I was seeking to know. Papochka's ghost knew and didn't precisely know what all he knew and what all he didn't know. He insisted that he always told the truth. What were his motivations? What did he want? Papochka knew one thing for sure: he had never told anyone that he wrote poetry and that he loved the sound of words and the rhythms of written expression and had always shown great prowess. A born poet, he'd win at anything he ever attempted to do, like writing sonnets, or making money, or bedding down a woman, or a man. Others would always lose. They would fail perpetually at anything and everything they tried. They sabotaged themselves. It wasn't fair either way. They didn't deserve to lose, and he didn't deserve to win all the time. But he did, and the fact he did made him appear invincible. (Would he let it slip who his real love was? No, he couldn't go that far, but I knew who it was. I was in love with him too.) I added that piece of knowledge or intuited information to my slowly emerging dream-like story of what the hell was going on. What was going on? Was it a tale to tell out of a dream?

"Why are you hiding your story in someone else's story?" Papochka had to know.

"Is that what I'm doing? Plagiarizing?"

"That or embedding, commandeering, misappropriating, hi-jacking another tale and burying yours just beneath the surface. So, when it's finished, readers will read a story and find you hidden there."

"A story-within-a-story."

"Hope you don't lose your way, son, on the quest for truth in your future writing," the apparition said. "Hope you can find the force of words to write your story when the time comes. Hope it is read, and hope you can escape criticism."

"In the past, before I retired from writing, if I failed," I said, "then I usually looked to find a new theme, or just another style, but the way was never lost; it was all part of truth-telling in the art of narration."

Suddenly, as in a dream, because it was a dream, we were in a dream room again, and the dream-room quickly filled up with surreal police agents coming through the windows and the doors and the walls, threatening us.

"The police agents," my papochka's apparition said. "We're under attack. We'll soon be under arrest. They want the lost and violent souls out of the land of the living. Even though I can't die twice, I must hurry back."

The demons apprehended and placed him forcibly under arrest and struggled to lead him away. The ghost transmogrified into the bodily form of Ilya, agitated, trembling, trying to escape. What could I do? Had the apparition been Ilya all along and not Papachka's ghost? It was my dream or dream vision, not unlike the tormented dreams of my past writing days when after a bad dream, I would be forced to write it down. I called after him: "Ilya, Ilya," but he had freed himself and would not stop running. All I could think to say was: "My runaway bride." What kind of dream was it? Plagiarized? Prophetic? Or both? Was my dream life imitating my real life, or the other way around? It was best to wake up and get back to taking the inside outside. I would have to make sense in my waking hours of this dream of appearance and reality from words, apparitions, ghostly forces, absence and myth, in remembering it, and, mostly from Ilya running away. The dream vision ended or was deferred. I woke up.

5th Dose

Finale (of sorts), or a False Ending, Really a New Beginning

It would be (or might be, or could be) tomorrow or tomorrow or another tomorrow in another century. Yes, as long as it took, but in haste to meet the need of my impetuous sense of time, everything had to be prepared quickly or hidden away. We cleaned up the mess and the mess of our mess in the aftermath of such anarchy, the indecency of taking everything outside and taking the outside in. Mamochka thought of us as conspirators, enemies of order and what was right and true.

"Things belong where they belong," she said, "and not in a confused mess of interchanging one thing for another."

New furnishings were ordered: she ordered them. Old ones were discarded, carted off and away. The wedding party was planned. (We planned it.) Musicians were hired. Mamochka had hired them, same ones as before, and then ordered to dig themselves into suitable and practicable holes, like good soldiers dug into trenches, entrenched deep enough to appear buried alive and yet shallow enough for them to play their instruments as if from underground. Four trumpets, 1 horn, 4 trombones, 1 tuba, additional parts for piccolo trumpet, horn in E-flat, trombones in treble clef and E-flat bass, if the music called for them. All of the players were dug in, buried, more or less, to various degrees. Not to mention, Fartovich, the conductor, up to his waist. Perverse? Punishing? Vengeful? Yes, this suited me. It was retributive justice for Taras, that is, Ilya. No police, though. No authorities. Roubles under the table would make them do whatever Mamochka wanted them to do. They did it.

She was to present us with rings made of white gold. Heavenovsky, as best man, would be forced to recite: "And they were married next day by the turkey that lived on the hill." Mamochka would conclude with: "For the sake of this company, to join this *man* and this *man* in love." With all of us, including Nina (the other witness and maid of honour) chanting: "'And they danced by the light of the moon. They danced by the light of the moon.'"

We wanted vengeful wedding music to march in with the "I-Do's," and an off-key hint of musicians struggling to breathe, planted as they were in the ground. But, according to the Gogolian laws of human oddity and absurdity, and how things turn out, it did not go quite as planned. Yes, the summerhouse was set to rights. Order prevailed: a place for everything and everything in its proper place. Of course, we planned the solemnities and we even ordered the sweetmeats and prepared for an outdoor luncheon, if the rain held off. I would be dressed all in white, so would the other bridegroom. Mamochka took out the ceremonial robes she loved to wear for weddings. We gathered. Mamochka took her place. So did Nina. I stepped out, shining. We waited. No sign of Heavenovsky: "late as ever" was how Nina put it. Still, there was no sign of Ilya (alias Taras) either. We continued to wait. The band sweltered in the heat. The sounds they made were subterranean. They were ordered (I ordered them) to stop torturing their noisy instruments and the hurt ears of the wedding party.

I was on the point of asking Nina to see where the other two were, especially Ilya. I was slightly concerned about a possible twist in the tale. Then Heavenovsky ambled across the lawn, dressed in a corn blue suit. Sheets of paper, held pincer-like between index and thumb, flapped lightly in the breeze. He looked up, froze, and then carried on, heading right for us.

"He's not coming," he said.

"Nerves, jitters?" I asked.

"Change of mind," he said.

"Yes, well, he has been through quite an ordeal. He is traumatized. Confused. He accepted, though. Agreed."

"He knew you would say that. He made me write down a message for you from him. I acted as secretary to a former secretary. We both liked that."

"Well, get on with it. Where is he?"

"Gone."

"He stood me up. Left me at the altar?"

"Stood you up, yes, and left you at the altar."

"Disgraced me. Shamed me."

"Shamed you, disgraced you, if that is how you feel it."

"Shut up and speak."

Heavenovsky plucked the first sheet from the others.

"Don't shoot the *mess*."

"Hurry up or I'll shoot you anyway."

He read on: "Dearest Anton, I cannot attend my own wedding. I cannot marry you or anyone. I was always in love with your papochka. He asked me to look after you. I did my best until I was buried alive. Yes, I said 'Yes' to your proposal. But I was under duress (underground) and would have said pretty much anything to escape my grave, to live, to be free. Not that I didn't feel the beauty of what you were proposing, even in the face of the current ban in our country. Still, for you and for all those in this summerhouse, marriage is a farce, and love is a game, in and out of love once a day. Here, vows are not vows but words uttered with fingers crossed behind your backs. To love (whatever that means), honour (if it suits you), and disobey (who obeys anyone anymore without force?). You play at love with the need to be mutually unhappy. Your expectations are perverse. There is no sanctity, no commitment that lasts a lifetime in your false conception of love and marriage. It is a sham and a dangerous game. Do you do things in love, in the name of love, in the acts of love? You come together only to separate, to hurt each other, dreaming of still others you wish you had met or could be with now, instead of the one you are with. You love that person when he/she is not there. When she/he is there, you don't. I played that game, too, until I met your papochka, Anton. We fell in love. He desecrated his own marriage vows to be with me, living a secret life, hurting Zoya, twisting you this way and that to continue to hurt her on his behalf beyond the grave. But you can't bury one and pluck out another. Do you remember your *Romeo and Juliet*? Who cares about them in this day and age? I do. Death is *not* the game-changer, the deal-breaker or dealmaker. Love is. Love is both. Love is all. You don't know how many tears I have shed, or blood I have shed, or will spill. I don't know how many tears you have cried, how much blood you've given for love. No more betrayals. No more punishing each other over the smallest things. No more making up. No more marriages, just as the Englishman said."

Heavenovsky, hurt, looked up from his 'script.'

"Don't stray or improvise, Heavenovsky," I said. "I can see that haunted look in your rat's eyes. You want to quote *Hamlet* at this point.

Do it, but only if you are prepared to be thrashed. (Here I raised my cane.) Otherwise, just read what is written."

Heavenovsky went on, reciting:

"But in your papochka's poem, he says: 'On the Fidgety Surface of Everyday Life: Love sustains itself and serves no special interest or purpose merely for its unintentional sake; and it is sufficient unto itself, because it cannot teach what it does not know, and has not been learned, and serves no master, and will not be master even of itself, because love is a manifesto of intimate words whispered, spoken, offered or written to the God of Love.'"

Heavenovsky took that sheet and placed it beneath the others, while shedding some like leaves with trembling, clumsy hands. But valiantly he read on:

"You act as if your lovers are your enemies. The real enemy of love is in your own heart. Instead of giving it away, you want to eat your enemy's heart."

"I can't believe that he would have said that, or any of it," I said. "You're making it up as you go along. Let me see those sheets. You didn't take dictation. You invented. This is your revenge on us for your failure in bed with Nina. He would never have said anything so obvious… so plagiarized. You're the only plagiarist here, Heavenovsky. Give me those pages."

Pages were flung in the air. Nina gathered them.

"Blank. Blank. Blank."

"A ploy, a fraud," I said. "You *are* a plagiarist."

"I embellished a bit," he said. "We talked; he confided in me. Gave me his story. Asked me to stand in for him, like his double, to make his case; get his point across, and give you his message. I gave him the keys to my car so that he could flee. He also wanted me to give you *this*."

"What is it: a love letter, a document, some secret revealed?"

"The great reveal?" asked Mamochka.

"It is a fragment of your papochka's autobiography," Heavenovsky said, "copied out in his secretary's hand that he wants you to read."

"Now?"

"No, not now: that would stop the flow."

"What flow, you idiot?"

"Of events as they are unfolding. Read it, he said, sometime after this episode in your life story."

"Episode?"

"The part of the story where you lose your lover."

"Give me that, before I rip your arm off with it and beat you with the wet end."

The autobiography changed hands only to be read (by me and others) after this episode.

"He also told me to say anything I wanted as long as I said he would *not* be getting married today."

"Or any other day," a shout came from the terrace, then a gunshot.

Taras/Ilya held up a pistol, took aim and fired again. This time, it ricocheted off the trumpet bell of the startled trumpet player. A mad scramble ensued among the musicians (or whoever they really were) to get out of their holes. They looked like confused soldiers coming under fire.

"He'll kill them all," I declared. "Ilya, Taras, whatever your name is, for pity's sake, stop shooting, even though they deserve to die for what they did to you. We'll avenge the outrage you had to endure in another way, not like this. Come down now. Let's get married as we planned to, and get away from all this absurdity. We'll go to St. Petersburg."

"You hate me," he said.

"No I don't. I love you."

"He hates *me*, Taras, not you," Mamochka said, "just as his papochka hated me and loved you. Come down. Put the gun down before it is too late."

"Yes, he hates his mamochka," Taras (Ilya) said. "But it's not natural, is it? He hates Heavenovsky, too, a poor poet who is harmless, only someone striving to love and work, despite lack of talent, lack of any gift whatsoever. He (Anton) despises Nina as well. But she is lost, a hopeless romantic, looking here and there for a perfect love, which doesn't exist, except with herself. He hates life as if you can take the inside out and outside in. He deplores the world. Therefore, he hates me (or will) in time. He thinks our love is a protest against life, an adolescent rebellion against convention. Privilege and entitlement, entitlement and privilege (P. E. E. P.) are responsible for your indolence, sloth, and indifference to the pain of others."

"I suffer because you suffer," I said. "Is that not enough? I can change. I can join you in a common cause."

"Once during a theatrical evening in the capitol," Ilya said, "someone called out to the performers on stage, denouncing them, exposing the fraud they were apparently perpetrating, saying: 'Here comes the parade of abominations.'[5] I never found out who the heckler was or what exactly he meant, but I've always remembered his words, this critic in the darkened theatre, and I owe him a debt of gratitude for his sentiment and his perfect sentence. So I say to you: I'll not join your parade of abominations."

"Then shoot *me*," I broke out. "Kill me for love. I'll die on my wedding day."

"You won't die today," he said, "not by my hand."

"I'll change," I said. "I'll keep changing into anyone or anything you want. I'll evolve."

"People like you don't change," he said, taking aim. "You only reveal yourselves."

"Reveal? Reveal what?"

"What you have hidden from others for so long," he said.

He kept shooting, trying to wound or kill the instruments as the musicians fled looking for cover. Then they began to return fire. Their concealed weapons were out in the open now.

"They're not musicians," Heavenovsky said. "Or not only musicians but *also*."

"Secret police," Taras/Ilya broke out.

He counted off the bullets and the last round until the chamber was empty. Then threw the pistol at the conductor fleeing from the barrage. In a strange turn, the gun bounced off a low wall and a piece of it hit the conductor's bleeding hand. The musicians took up positions with their weapons to return fire. It was not friendly.

"Goodbye, Anton, forget me." Ilya said. "I'll do everything I can to forget you."

"Where are you going? You'll be shot dead if you run for it."

"I'm going to test an *Idea*."

"What idea?"

"Whether the State is right and I am wrong or whether I am right and the State is wrong."

"I'll go with you. We'll test it together."

"The *Idea* doesn't include you."

"Please, I want to be with you."

"Not now."

"When?"

---

5   The heckler that shouted in the dark theatre was identified as a wit named A. Oliveira.

"I don't know. It all depends on whether I'm right or wrong, and whether I'll live to talk about it."

Taras (aka Ilya), wounded, disappeared from view. Had he jumped to his death, the way my papochka had? It appeared so except for the fact that Mamochka spotted him limping into a waiting car (Heavenovsky's) and driving off. Were we now safe from the *assassin, turned fugitive?* Mamochka took charge. She stepped closer to me, slipped her arm through mine as if in a ligature. It felt like a house arrest.

"It will be all right, son," she said, "no matter what happens next. We'll just start again. No more hating, especially your mamochka. Love me as I love you, and let's start over again."

Nina stepped closer to Heavenovsky with the blank sheets held up to him, and he crumpled them into a fistful of paper.

"Your greatest piece of writing, Valentin," she said.

"My blank masterpiece," he said. "I'll likely be arrested before I can sign it."

"Love is your theme," she said.

"Our theme, my love. It should cure anyone of the need for a certain kind of love. Love's remedy is the willingness to 'start over.' Can we start again? Try again?"

"Can we really believe we are capable of ever truly loving each other?" she asked, or I thought she did. "More to the point, can we ever leave each other?"

"Who would have us? *Neither with you, nor without you* is closer to the truth."

"Why do we do this to each other? Is this what love is?"

"We do it because it is what is expected: *the course of true love* and all that."

"Smoothness or roughness is one thing, madness is another."

"We're doomed to be together, then, totally madly in love with love, consumed like fire and powder."

"Ah, yes, as *they kiss consume.*"

They kissed as if to consume one another.

"They're going too far, as always," Mamochka said.

"One thing is certain," I said.

"One thing?"

"We all went too far."

"Too far, and how far is that, son?"

"Where we *are*."

"But is it better than where we will end up?"

"Time will tell, but it's not talking. Well, shall I look for the spent bullets in anticipation of the investigation?" I asked.

"We'll do it together," Mamochka said, "and in so doing, prepare our story or alibi."

"Better us than the police, Mamochka. Do you think those *musicians* will call the police?"

"Call the police? They are the police, Anton."

The dream had been prophetic.

"When they targeted Taras for his past political activities in which your papochka was also involved," Mamochka said, "they were trying to warn *you*, and so you see, they've also been watching me for some time now, interested to see if my 'marriage ceremonies' and my wild ideas about love and marriage run counter to the ban."

"Yes, *better* us, Mamochka," I said better *us* than the *police*."

6th Dose

The Vaccine Allergy

The police begged to differ. Only the secret branch of the police did not beg. They refused to beg. In fact, if anyone were to do the begging, it would not be the secret police. Interrogators do not beg. *You* beg, if you are the one being interrogated. The police had ugly questions that needed uglier answers. *Now.* Sooner rather than later, as it turned out. The answers to their questions would help them to determine how things would turn out in the end for all of us. Ending it was the point. In a dossier on the family, the investigators had a trove of photos, documents, and "evidence." Their surveillance of the place and the activities of those who came and went had an overarching purpose: to stomp on dissidents and to stamp them out, by first flushing out the dissidents promoting anti-government political and/or religious beliefs counter to the bans and laws and then making them beg for mercy. Violence was not necessarily the last option. Compliance was not always of interest to the authorities. Torture was the dealmaker. They knew what was going on at the Antonov place with Mamochka's "marriage ceremonies."

They also knew what her son (me) was doing. They had my own words to use against me in my own writings. Too bad "manuscripts did not burn." Had they been I, they would have tried to burn them. They also knew who and what Ilya (aka Taras) was and what he was up to, the real dissident and the kind of true and subversive dissidence that required extreme means to quell it. They also had information about my papochka. He was safely out of the way now. His own words had condemned him, despite the twisted and self-indulgent nature of his writing. They had already read his "autobiographical" work, the same one that I would read on the night that Ilya had left me and run off, being pursued by secret policemen, who were also hired musicians. I waited to read it (the same one that the police had already read, interpreted and filed away).

When I finally read it, it was like getting jabbed, that is to say, inoculated against the unforeseen, and I said to no one in particular because no one else was there: "So much for my papochka and his conception of the world, his world, thinking of himself as a figure in a work by M.C. Escher. Madness had done the work of a bullet in the back of the head, or a waste of Novichok, a military-grade chemical nerve agent, that could be used in the attack against any political activist, or decadent dissident, like my dead papochka."

7ᵗʰ Dose

Heavenovsky, Athol and Bagot

The police had also arrested and detained Heavenovsky and Nina as they left the summerhouse, swearing that they were married and off for a proper honeymoon. Were they accessories to Ilya's political activities and flight from justice? When asked, during an interrogation, which they later described to me in detail, where they had gone, and what they had done, Heavenovsky said that he and Nina had been *plucking flowers*.

"What are you talking about?"

His answer came in the form of a descriptive, lyrical passage, uninterrupted, because it was odd and therefore, self-incriminating. They had to record his confession anyway. Why not let him sing like a bird. He did.

"It was always a case of lovers meeting," he said, "lovingly entreating, but words were usually faltering and failing, despite the poet (me) poeticizing. The critics were cruelly and critically criticizing, and my versifying was frequently worsening. So Nina was yelling yeowling at me with me fearing her and yearning for something else. Both of us were longing for different lives. Then I was running away just as we got engaged. Nerves? Jitters? Not sure. Hearts breaking and broken, the affair was soul-destroying, if you can believe it. I made a fool of myself: hiding then seeking and finding a job. Imagine my surprise when who should come into my life again, carrying a cake in such a lovely and beguiling way, but Nina. I'm a poet. So let me use an image of plucking: a flower, a flower with many petals, a daisy, say, and as I pluck the petals, I say, 'She loves me, she loves me not, she loves me.' Well, when Nina takes the flower, not the same one I picked and plucked, but another, another daisy, say, with many petals, and she plucks them, saying, 'I hate him, I hate him not, I hate him." That is the crux of the matter, as I see it, the dilemma of our plucked and deflowered love. Do you see? Of course, I made a fool of myself, as I said. You can call me a fool. I deserve it. That is my crime. That is what brought me *here*."

They found his confession laughable, especially with the insistence of plucking flowers, and they laughed at their own laugh laughing at him. After his risible outpouring (a plagiarist's field day on a field of daisies), Heavenovsky was let go. Apparently, his interrogators had been highly entertained by his "flower image" or whatever it was, as proof of his complete incompetence as a human being, let alone a dissident. But Nina was detained for the time being. Heavenovsky protested as mildly as he could, but complied in the face of their cruel laughter, and went off to his little apartment in the city. Nina was kept in a holding cell for as long as they liked. They had a lot of time on their hands. The honeymooners were separated once again. Not seeing each other meant they were longing to. Heavenovsky vowed to get my mamochka to try to help secure Nina's release. But could Mamochka deal with the police, especially when she wanted to extricate me from the whole brutal farce? There was also the matter of a case they had against her and her son (me). Police? No police? What was the best thing to do? The last thing Heavenovsky remembered before being laughed out of the detention centre was asking to see Nina. Request: denied. But the interrogator said, half-smiling: "Don't worry, we'll take very good care of your young bride." That kind of 'care' horrified him.

As a trust of how Nina was being taken care of, two men examined her. They called themselves Athol and Bagot, as if they were British. It suited their techniques. It gave them masks to wear, roles to play. One mask could speak to another mask without revealing what was behind it. To remove the masks was to reveal that nothing was behind it: the true horror. Their masks were their faces.

"Tell us about your husband," the one who called himself Bagot said.

"What husband?" Nina wanted to know, not remembering much on purpose. "I haven't got a husband."

"That comes as a surprise," Athol said. "He said you were married. How quickly a beautiful, young woman forgets."

"*Were* married? Yes, that is, I don't know what to say. What do you want me to say?"

"What's it to do with us?"

"You're either married or single. Which is it?"

"Did all your previous husbands die on their wedding nights?"

"Previous? Well."

"He's playing with you, but you're used to playing and being played with, aren't you?"

"Well."

"You married or thought you did, and next day you wanted a divorce, am I right?"

"Well."

"Was it his *big mouth,* as he suggested, or his *little?*"

"Please stop. I don't know what you want me to say. You have obviously recorded or eavesdropped on everything we said and did without impunity. Our honeymoon was under surveillance. Is that legal? Why have you arrested me and brought me here? What have I done?"

"That's for us to figure out," the man who identified himself as Bagot said.

"It is easy to determine," the man who identified himself as Athol suggested. "We'll figure it out."

Then Heavenovsky, trying to protect Nina, and vainly attempting to defend himself with *words,* told the police agents that he understood that the marriage ceremony and the failed honeymoon attempt were strange (was that the right word?) rites of passage for him, but not for his bride. Was it not the word that someone (he thought it was Nina) had used: *strange?*

"Yet Nina did not like what she heard," Heavenovsky went on, going too far as usual. "When I said I didn't know what to say about my failure to pleasure her, Nina, broke out with: 'What else is there to say? You have said it all. Save your breath. I've tried everything with you to provoke the correct response and to get you to see what I want you to see. Sometimes, I wonder what I was doing with you at all. You've left me no choice,' she added.'"

The police agents began to laugh.

"She walked away," Heavenovsky continued, saying too much. "When I couldn't get her back, I began again. This time, I was alone, no help from Z. and her son, A. It became guesses and supposes I wasn't used to, but as in poetry, so, too, in love. My words, like my love life, collapsed. I don't want to say the word: *failed.* I realized that I had made a fool of myself."

"Like your love life. Yes, I like that."

"Yes, made a fool of yourself. I like that."

They decided to let him go, so amused were they at his statements that they knew he was the fool he took himself for, and hence innocent. Later, Heavenovsky was to tell Nina that they had let him go, because with his *surreal confession* he had made them laugh. He began to see humour as a form of escape, and comedy as a means of survival.

But though they released him, still laughing, they kept Nina there for two days, question after question, in non-stop rounds and volleys, most of which she could not answer, dared not answer, or would not. She prayed that someone on the outside would help to free her.

True to his word, Heavenovsky sought my mamochka's help in the matter. She may have been under suspicion, but she still had connections in the government. It would be a simple matter to get Nina out of trouble. Simple. Yes, but she would have to agree to permit her son, Anton (me), to get into a lot more trouble than Nina was ever in. This was the trade off. When one was let out, another was taken in. Mamochka agreed, but had already set up my defense, no matter what the charges were, and failing that, the escape. She was obsessed with rescuing me.

Nina was transported to Heavenovsky's apartment in the capitol. Into his waiting arms, the police-tormented bride collapsed. Her world had collapsed. She had gone too far again. Once again, she had made a fool of herself. In fact, just before she fell, Heavenovsky thought he heard her say: "What a fool." But what did she actually mean? Did she mean *herself* as in: "What a fool I am." Or Heavenovsky, as in: "What a fool *you* are." One thing was certain: it was either a reference to herself and her foolishness or to him and his folly.

"Otherwise," Heavenovsky said, not knowing where to put her body down, "she would have said: 'What fools we are, or what fools we have been.'" At least, he was able to conclude that since she did not mean him, in all likelihood, there was a chance that she still loved him. But would he make of fool of himself again, if she didn't?

"Yes," he said, answering his own ugly/beautiful question.

8ᵗʰ Dose

My Interrogators and Me

At first, I thought we were only talking (that was what they had said that they were doing with me, talking to me), but when they applied physical pressure, then I knew they weren't just talking anymore. With each provocation, each threat, allegation, intimidation, I resorted to words, words, words. What else could I do?

"You call yourselves Bagot and Athol," I said, "but when do police agents use Englishmen as interrogators."

"Maybe never."

"Maybe all the time."

"Maybe now, if that is what you would have me believe."

"What do you believe?"

"About what?" I asked. "The divine? Our social system? The origin of the word 'narcissism'?"

"All of the above, and marriage. What is your opinion of marriage?"

"Not you too. Why is everyone always asking me that question?"

"Who is always asking you that? Maybe, they are interested in your answer to see if it is the right answer."

"Or the wrong one."

"Let it be right. Let it be wrong."

"This is *not*."

"I know, *not* the U.S.A. or Europe. And we know what that means."

"What does it mean?"

"That this is a cozy chat with the secret police."

"Tell us your views of marriage."

"Views? I subscribe to the views of Andrei Bely."

"Who?

"That mystic, theosophist, novelist, poet from the turn of another century, Boris Bugaev."

"I'll look him up in our files. But for now, tell us what those views are and how they relate to you?"

I did until they stopped me when I said:

"Marriage should be mystical or not at all."

"Don't tell my wife that," one of them said.

"I won't," I said. "But when I was still reading philosophy, I read a philosopher on the subject of love and marriage. He characterizes the union of a man and a woman as a form of *mutual unhappiness*. Is there something fatal at the heart of matrimony that causes its breakdown?"

"Which philosopher?" the other one wanted to know.

"Well, Denis de Rougemont in *Love in the Western World*."

"Right, right in the West, but not the East."

"But."

"We're not here to philosophize with you."

"But you're trying to frighten me," I said.

"Are you afraid for something you did not commit?"

"No, for something I may have committed by means of my personal views on marriage."

I came within a hairsbreadth of telling them that all marriage, successful ones and failures alike, are likely based on a *lie*. Fundamentally, one or both have their fingers crossed at the altar. That kind of deceit, concealment, and treachery forced me to believe that there should be *no more marriages*. I was quoting. (Who did I think I was: Heavenovsky?) One had cheated or wanted to; one had a lover or longed to; or they had to marry with a shotgun or pitchfork at their backs. Even if the lie were never revealed, even after a lifetime together, it would fester and end up with no intimacy and no words: a deep silence like a chasm opens up between a man and a woman, yearning to be somewhere else, and longing to be with someone else. The lie is that they think that they can be happily married. The truth is mutual unhappiness, as in Strindberg's *Dance of Death, Part I*. Just look at any wedding portrait and see if the mystery of their married love can be discerned and/or revealed. How will it end? They have made a mistake, a costly one, a soul-destroying mistake. Was I pessimistic? A pessimist? Or was I just a cynic? Was I cruel and heartless? Were my opinions a biting critique of marriage and its breakdown? Was it just a sad, disturbed and cynical patchwork of resentment? No, I wanted marriage to be *true*. Again, I was expressing a literary concept as in Shakespeare's "the marriage of true minds," or Christian romanticism as in "two shall become one." Was I just a frustrated idealist? I was frustrated. That was true. Well, that was what I had wanted to say to the police agents, but it was best, under the circumstances, not to talk about it. Besides, I knew they wanted to trap me: make me reveal my own sexuality, my own preference in defiance of the current ban. Did it really interest them the "way" I did sex or wanted to? What could they do? No one was sent to the northern regions in this day and age; at least, I didn't think so. Detention? A prison term in a prison colony? My mamochka would take care of it, if it came to that. She took care of everything else, didn't she? What was a mamochka for but to protect you and arrange things and wriggle you out of trouble when you got into it? All I wanted now was freedom. I wanted to be free to pursue Ilya and to help him and to love him, as I always had. Our love was our freedom. We did not have to marry. That is, not now, not here, anyway; some other time, maybe, and some other place. The West, maybe, if we could get out.

"Does your mamochka perform secret marriages?" Athol asked.

"Ask her," I said.

"We intend to," Bagot said. "But isn't that what you yourself called them?"

"A joke. I was joking, jesting. It was a quip."

"A joker, a jester, of course. Is it natural to joke about a mamochka? What kind of a son-of-a-bitch quips about his mamma?"

Would words ever be a counterforce to the power of interrogation and state oppression? Could I joke my way out of this situation? There had been famous cases in history, albeit literary history. Here I thought of the trials of Oscar Wilde. What was the result? "We often kill the thing we love" as in the "Ballad of Reading Gaol," and humiliation, exile and more."

"Look," I said, "my mamochka would marry anyone to anyone else. She believes in the benefits of matrimony: perhaps, because her own marriage was a shambles, a complete failure. My papochka neglected her from what I understand; betrayed her. No intimacy, no respect. He cheated on her with his secretary."

"A male *amanuensis with special privileges*?"

"All right, yes. She hid her sorrows, for the sake of being married to my papochka; and I suppose for my sake as well. Now, she is a high priestess for all, a Mamochka-to-Us-All. She has a syndrome that I call "Clan Identification: C.I."

They showed interest in my notion of identification.

"C.I.: Clan Identification?"

"Yes, it's different from honouring one's clan or ancestors."

"What is the problem with it?"

"As I see it," I said, "my mamochka identifies with other people's clans to the point where she thinks she is part of those clans. They think the world of her. She never asks anything of them. Instead, she gives and gives to the point of self-sacrifice. The danger comes when her identification with her own clan or family comes into conflict with the clan values of others. She is divided. She must act according to her clan's wishes, but cannot in defiance of the wishes of others. Try living with that type of person, generous to a fault, but always blaming you for tension with other folks. You are being true to yourself and your clan's needs, but she thinks you are stirring up trouble when those needs come into conflict with the need and greed of others."

"But what's wrong with clan loyalty?"

"And how does it relate to the question of your views on marriage?"

"Well, yes, it is a part of our history, including discrimination and violence, and is the basis of marriage ceremonies and bringing peace between warring clans. My mamochka wants all clans to intermarry. This means *offspring*, which means fertility rites, which means that those with a *different*."

"Orientation."

"Orientation, yes. They do not fit into her concept of life."

"*You*, for example."

"Me, for *example*."

"And you admit it."

"I do."

"Brave *or*."

"Stupid. There are virtues in being stupid *but*."

"Not in being naive and reckless."

"Has she ever performed same-sex marriages as in the West?"

"Not in my presence."

"Has she ever agreed to perform such a marriage?"

"Well, it was not performed."

"Yours and the fugitive? He has one of the most dangerous heads in the state."

"Dangerous head? As dangerous as a potato, I think," I said, "and therefore, not dangerous at all."

"Thankfully, your mamochka did not get a chance to perform the union."

"We'll be sure to pursue this point with her in our conversation. Thank you for your insights and disclosure."

"She thinks she's the eternal feminine, don't you see?" (I suddenly couldn't stop talking. Somebody had to listen to me, but why the secret police?). "She identifies with others to the point where all young people are her children; all families are her families; all husbands are her secret husbands. Make of it what you will."

"Secret husbands? I'll make a note. She wanted *you* married."

"Yes."

"To a *woman*?"

"So this is what it's about and what it comes round to in a cyclical way?" I asked. "It comes out at last. If so, it is bound to drag on."

"You're a discerning man. We know about your membership to a certain club (clandestine). They appear to be world-haters, women-haters, and life-haters. But they are *cocksmen* all the same."

"Am I a cocksman? Why should anyone demonize me? Am I not a man, and the man you refer to as 'the fugitive' is he not a man? Are we merely body parts, our private parts, say, attaining consciousness, impersonating us, walking away to live a separate life; or a nose, say, that has detached itself or has been cut off from our faces, and goes about with our names and identities, our consciousness, and leaves us deprived of our noses?"

"He is alluding to "The Nose" by Gogol?"

"A literary allusion from a literary man," Bagot said. "But if he mentions "The Double" by Dostoyevsky, I'll throw the book at him."

"Your point?" Athol demanded.

"Am I not a man," I said, "and not just a body part?"

"If you are a man, then be one."

"Be a man, and do what is lawful."

"As we see it, based on our surveillance of your actions, you live an inverted life. Your world is upside down. You should love your mamochka, but, contrary to natural feeling, you can't stand her. You do handstands to prove that you'd rather stand on your head than on your feet, the right way around. When your mamochka asked you what you are doing, you say that you are "standing on my head, like Father William in *Alice's Adventures in Wonderland.*" You should obey your country's laws and the bans, but you are always ready to defy them. You should get married, but you invert it and, some would say, *pervert* the laws of nature, to choose otherwise. You can't leave things as they are, can you? You take the inside outside and the outside in. Absolute inversion."

"Inversion? I like that," I said. "I defy the laws, even those of gravity, because the world is upside down with prejudice and discrimination, and because that is how I am made."

"Made or unmade, remake yourself or else."

It was about the little matter of the ban on anything that contravened traditional values. Athol and Bagot agreed to let me go on two prickly but simple conditions. There would be no need to involve my mamochka, provided I helped them entrap Ilya. They even offered me a state-owned weapon to carry out the arrest (shoot him if I got the chance or had to or myself if it ever became necessary) or bring him in at gunpoint, if it came to that. I seemed to be given control over my lover's life and even his death.

"Agreed?"

How could I refuse? My world was inverting, collapsing, words tumbling down around my ears, ideas in ruins. I had made a fool of myself, and what was the supreme irony that I was becoming more and more like Heavenovsky. When they let me go, I realized that I had never carried or even handled a gun before.

PART FOUR

*The Cure for Love as Prescribed by
the Police Agents*

1ˢᵗ Dose

Ilya's Solo

All I knew about the condition of my beloved fugitive was that Ilya was bleeding from a gunshot wound to the leg. He was driving Heavenovsky's cheap car as *fast* as he could. I didn't like it, but I didn't know why I didn't like it. The speed of his thoughts likely outdistanced the miles he travelled. Was he thinking what I thought he was thinking? What was he thinking about? Was he thinking about me at all? This was what I thought he was thinking, or thought he might be thinking about:

"I know that I won't escape pursuit this way, and that I'll likely be caught or killed in this getaway attempt. I didn't kill anyone, but only wounded a few damaged musical instruments. Still. I have to hide. I have enemies (especially among the secret police), but I also have friends. I've devoted years of my life to helping others. I'll have to find safe passage out of the country near N—. I've always looked out for the less fortunate. I've loved country folks all my life and aided them whenever I could, especially with legal matters. I've always been keen on causes, especially in helping to 'liberalize' our society. I've helped the less fortunate and assisted dissidents to escape police action.

"My intimate relationship with Anton's papochka was not only personal but also political. We loved each other and fought for rights near and dear to our own hearts. Freedom was the goal, then: freedom in all areas of life and personal conduct, especially in the matter of love and sex. We clashed with the laws and the bans. We were at odds with the prevailing views on sex. The jury is still out on Anton's papochka's demise. He had been provoked and cornered because of a political matter that involved only me. Since they could not get me, they 'got' my patron and my lover. It had been ruled a suicide, but I know better. The man loved life, despite his fanatical views of how it should be lived. He had hurt his wife, Zoya, by betraying her. I've always felt remorse for what she must have suffered. But I've dedicated myself to helping Anton until one day I realized that Anton was in love with me as his papochka had been before. Impossible situation, but my life story is full of such situational impossibilities. I have to get away from the police, and also from Anton. I don't want more Antonov blood on my hands. I'm in a crisis."

That was what I thought that he was likely thinking. It suited my purposes, and I wanted him to think and feel that way.

2ⁿᵈ Dose

My Solo

Awkwardly armed with a gun and my swordstick, I actually drove my mamochka's car (I hated driving and I was a bad driver) to the place I knew Ilya to be:

"The little farmhouse outside the town of N—. I want to turn the tables on the police and rescue my beloved. I think I've bought time and a supervised freedom. I know I'm likely leading the police right to Ilya. Still, there are virtues to being stupid, but not to being ignorant. It is like playing dead. Just as there are virtues to madness, until you go mad or encounter true insanity. I'll think of some way, even a shootout, if I can get the gun to work and if it has bullets."

When I was in the country, I rolled down the window, took the pistol and fired into a farmer's field. The blast and the report detonated in my ears and terrified me.

"Now I know it's loaded, but with one bullet less. How many are still in the chamber? I'll have to wait to find that out. I hope that there is at least one bullet left. But I won't worry about that now as I travel into the dark interior.

"Fortunately, I have two bottles of vodka with me in the front seat, one for myself and the other for Ilya to drink and pour on his wounds. Of course, why didn't I take a first-aid kit to clean and dress the wounds? Will my lover bleed to death? Is he dead already? Stupidity, madness, and neglect: the inside has been taken outside. I realize now that I belong in the interior and not out in the open. The exterior is a menace, a threat. The interior is my hiding place, a place I can control with language. I have words for the inside, not for the outside. Those trees, for example, what are they called? Those birds, do I know the names of birds? Even the names of villages and towns are strange to me, despite having seen them on maps. I'll take Ilya to someplace *inside* away from the hostility of the wide-open spaces. I never realized before how agoraphobic I really am. At least, my room is a womb, a safe haven. Dammit, I can never get away from my mamochka, the eternal feminine."

3ʳᵈ Dose

Mamochka and Two Sympathetic Interrogators

Athol and Bagot took the interrogation inside: into the summerhouse. (I was able to view the exchange on the playback from the surveillance tapes later on. What I could not make out, I filled in the gaps with my writer's imagination.) My momochka had friends in high places. She had served the state. She was an agent. This would be a conversation. She got to the point as soon as her guests sat down, drinks in hand, smiling.

"Leave *them* alone," she said. "Let them go. I'll get them out. They can go to Germany, or Norway. They can travel to France or Italy. Maybe, they will like North Africa, or Canada. Or anywhere they can live together. If they do anything to embarrass me, or, more to the point, our society, you know there are ways to stop them, silence them, make them suffer, punish them, with a punishment worse than imprisonment or even death."

"We know," Bagot said.

"You know we know," Athol smiled.

"So?"

"We're following your son. He knows it. We're giving him time. He agreed to find the fugitive."

"He doesn't know what he agreed to, the fool," my mamochka said. "You gave him a pistol?"

"Well."

"We gave him a gun and a bullet or two."

"He'll likely shoot himself by accident," she said. "He knows nothing from nothing. All he knows is from books. I've looked after him, taken care of him. He has betrayed me more than his papochka ever did, although in many other ways. But I've never abandoned him. I've watched over him, hoping against hope that one day he would mature. Be a man. The kind of man I want him to be. But he is immature, still a boy, despite his age, a parasite, always taking, never giving, always proselytizing, always using words where only deeds will do. Let the boy and his friend go. Let them go on a world tour: *lune de miel.* Let them see what the world really is, and a honeymoon. Let's watch them to see if they ever grow up."

"What about his impulses, his orientation?" Athol asked.

"His problem is that he wants love to be true," she said. "Is that a crime?"

"It is if it contradicts the ban," Bagot said. "The law."

"Yes, when rights come into conflict with rites. Only *here.*"

"No, not only here but everywhere where accepted laws of nature are upheld by tradition and custom in honour of fertility and destiny and are held as sacred, legal. Do what you do in secret, but why cry about it when you're caught?"

"He must be cured of his illness, an illness which is illicit love."

"I think he wants to blow up his identity."

"Yes, he wants to blow up his nationality."

"He is dynamite that wants to blow up natural laws, state laws, and reality."

"He wants to blow up his mamochka. But he is a talker. It is his mouth that gets him into trouble. He is just a mouth and not a complete man. But please, do as I ask."

"We can't do as you suggest," Bagot said.

"We can't do it, as you know. But if they get away," Athol added, "we'll do what we can within strict limits to cover their tracks and conceal their flight. We may be interrogators, but we are sympathetic sons, especially to a mamochka like you. We really don't care about how he does sex. It is the fugitive we want for past crimes. We'll back off your son."

"But only for a short period of time, Zoya," Bagot said.

"You'll have to buy him that time, but even a short time is very expensive."

"I want the fugitive apprehended for this, and also for all he and my late husband did to me. But please wait," she said. "I'll pay."

"We'll wait."

"We'll wait to be paid."

4ᵗʰ Dose

Ilya and Me

We faced each other once the farmhand had put down his weapon and gone back into the barn at Ilya's request.

"I thought you up these past hours and there you are," Ilya said looking in all six directions.

"You've been on my mind, too," I said, breathlessly, "I can assure you, and here you are. I knew where you would be. You see how well I know you. We have a past."

"We're just thoughts in each other's heads. The past is not the future."

"They think we're mad."

"Everyone thinks so. If this is mental illness, what's the cure?"

"Decriminalization? Acceptance? Don't ask, and don't tell?"

"No cure."

"You're in my heart, Ilya. You know I still can't bring myself to call you that."

"Call me what you want, but hurry. One of us has to go now."

"I came to be with you, look after you, take you away, get away from here. Blow this place up, this life, our past identities, and turn things around."

"The gunshot wound has been looked after," Ilya said. "I have friends here. They knew what to do. But your coming here has jeopardized us all. You must know that if they let you come, they've been following you."

"Yes, but I think I bought some time, though. I thought we could outwit them. They're not too bright. I suppose they don't have to be when they are brute or sly force. I foisted them off on my mamochka. She'll know what to do, what to say, and how to get us out of this mess."

"The mess of your mess, Anton, but not this time. I'm going alone. I'm going on alone until I drop."

Ilya pulled out his gun. On impulse, I withdrew my weapon, my hand trembling. Would I shoot? If I didn't, would I get shot?

"Is this a standoff? A shootout? A duel?" I asked him. "I love you. How can I be expected to shoot you?"

"I love you, too, but I'll shoot you, if I have to."

"What happened to you, Ilya? To us?"

"I had a moral crisis," he said. "You must understand that I fell from grace. I fell. Being short, I didn't have far to fall. I denied those that denied me. But still felt betrayed. Betrayed by those with divided loyalties. They could not choose. They certainly couldn't choose *me*. Then I began to fall into a crisis of conscience. I knew what was going on all around me. I yelled, jumped up and down, made myself sick trying to call out the wickedness I saw, but no one wanted to listen. They had listened enough. Enough. So I stopped talking. When I didn't speak, there was only silence. When I didn't act, there was only motionlessness. No words. No intimacy. No movement. So I decided to fall down."

As if to prove his point, he went down on one knee, taking better aim at me.

"Get up, get up, Ilya," I begged. "I'm here. I'll help you as I did to get you out of that grave. You're alive. We're still alive. Ilya, I love you. Talk to me. Touch me. Get up off the ground."

He stood up. I was in his sights. Ilya then looked up quickly. He heard, as I did, the whirring of helicopters.

"They're here," he said. "It will be over soon. It will be a helicopter ending as in a bad movie. I'll keep walking backwards to give you time to get into your car and go back home. If you don't move, Anton, I'll start shooting until you do. Or kill you, if you don't."

"I'm willing to die for love," I said, "in a hail of bullets, or is it gunfire?"

"Die for true love, yes," he said, "but not for romance and romantic illusion."

"Then you don't love me."

"In my own way, I do. But I also love *humanity*. You don't."

"I want to marry you."

"Yes, as a provocation to others, a protest against traditional values and as a gesture, but it is only for yourself, not for others, and certainly not for *me*."

"You want to save the world," I said. "I just want to hide in my corner of it. We were not meant to be out here. It terrifies me, but inside. My life is interior. Interiority defines me."

"I love people that are desperate, that are suffering, that need freedom."

"I had not realized what a moralist you really were, a preacher of a dead gospel, a revolutionary without weapons."

"I'm a social preacher, all right. My vision of social justice is my weapon. And I must act on what I see and know."

"Act on our love, Ilya. Let's go before it is too late."

"It's too late, Anton. As I was struggling to live in that hole, my grave, I thought of how desperate others are in the world, suffocating, trapped, while in your summerhouse all there is is silliness, absurdity, and farce. But the farce is over. The curtain falls now."

I pulled the trigger. Blank. I tried again. Nothing. It was at that point that two black helicopters swooped down, like giant dragonflies.

"Shoot at the whirligigs," Ilya shouted. "Shoot."

"No ammo," I broke out, hurling the gun into the air as if to hit the helicopter and bring it down as in a helicopter ending.

"You were set up," he said. "They wanted you to shoot yourself, even in the foot, and me, even by accident. They want us to shoot each other, the deader the better for all concerned. Can't you see who is behind it all?"

"My mamochka?"

"Yes, she is an agent. Your papochka and I were trying to expose her. She exposed him. They pressured him until he did himself in. I was working to strip away all her deceptions and lies, treachery and the rest. Never mind. Quick, run for cover. The farmhands will come to our aid if I ask them to, but it will mean bloodshed. She was trying to get a fix on Heavenovsky. Yet he is not a subversive, but an inept poet and a self-blinding romantic. At least, he's not a dead one."

"Will we be?"

5ᵗʰ Dose

End of the Farce (sort of)

Something like a brief firefight ensued. The farmhands did their best against the heavily armed police, but were stopped. Mamochka emerged from one of the choppers, dressed in black leather, in charge of the operation. It was a helicopter ending, but with one's mamochka in charge of the arrest. Ilya and I were apprehended. My dilemma, apart from the issue with Ilya, was: "Do you call the arresting officer 'Mamochka' during the arrest?"

"Let us *go*, Mamochka," I pleaded. "Leave us be. We've done no harm."

"You've been saved from it," she said.

"What are you going to do to us?"

"What do you want to do, son?"

I stared at the wounded and restrained Ilya.

"Go home, provided you let Ilya go anywhere he wants to go. Let him go to any border he wishes and release him."

"Don't you want to marry him?"

"Yes, but I have to convince him first, and he must stay alive to consider me, and the ban can't last forever, can it? Anyway, I want him to live."

"You love him that much?"

"Touching," either Bagot or Athol said.

"I'll see what I can do for him," Mamochka said.

"What about me?"

"You'll always have your mamochka."

"Ilya will go on forever travelling and wandering in search of justice for all the downtrodden and misbegotten. He will not return. He will see the world. But for me, I must go back."

"You must, Anton, and when you do, you'll see your familiar world. Also, I've invited Heavenovsky and Nina to stay with us. They need my help to correct and then perfect their married love."

"Returning to the same place to where we started. In doing so, I see the abomination of desolation. In my return to my room, to my beloved inside and all that is interior and within, I go back to the abomination, desolate, alone."

"You'll have me, son."

"That's exactly what I'm afraid of," I said. "You'll put me in a maternal cage."

"If I do, you'll only rattle the bars. There, I'm giving it back to you in your own brand of humour."

"What is funny, but not really, is that Ilya had his hole; while I have my mamochka, both buried alive."

"If you're calling your mamochka an abomination," Bagot or Athol said, "I'll throw you out of the chopper myself. She went to a lot of trouble to extricate you from the mess you made with that Ilya."

"No, no, he doesn't mean that," Mamochka said. "He's a writer and uses and abuses words for their sound and fury. He *means*. What do you mean, Anton?"

"Nothing."

"That's right, he means nothing by it. *Abomination* is just a word, and he loves words most of all, like his dead papochka."

"I love them most of all, next to the fugitive," I said.

"Well, yes, we all have someone or something we love more than something or someone else. You loved doing *nothing* and criticizing everything."

"I was not (and am not) Oblovmov, Mamochka. This thing started with something out of a Chekhov farce and nearly ended with Dostoevsky's *Crime and Punishment*. But it is really Gogol who triumphs here. We're all just fools, mortally so."

"A bit of a stretch, Anton, for those of us who do not like literature or literary allusions, or those of us who find that you are reducing everything to absurdity."

"*Reduction* is the point," I said. "To expose the lies, the prejudices. Never mind. I forgot what I was going to say. Suffering is not literary criticism."

"How do you feel, Anton," Mamochka asked, leaning close.

"As if I've been slapped," I said.

"A moral slap?" she wanted to know. "That is, a correction for your immature act."

"A Gogolian slap in the face of love and its pretensions," I said. "It's all *poshlust (poshlost)*."

"Whichever it is, let's go home," she said.

"*Home* is another word," I said, "that I'm not sure of, like a dose of bitter-tasting medicine for an incurable malady."

"Yes, *home, Anton,* where you belong. You'll rest, heal, regroup and figure out what to do from there."

"That's what I'd call a grotesque kick in the backside of my fate. For all the forty years of my loud-mouthed clowning, I guess I was never a complete person. I was just a *mouth,* after all: a mouth that had inexplicably attained consciousness and was living the absurd life of a selfish man."

6ᵗʰ Dose

Second False Finale in a Second Attempt to End the Absurdity

Home? Home was the abomination of desolation in my enforced return: I felt desolate, alone, despite the company, and with my lover outside, somewhere in the country. I had returned home. Heard the admonitions. Was forced to listen. Listened enough. Since I could not sleep, I read my papochka's quasi-allegorical autobiography: *The Fictional Autobiography of Sergei Antonovich Antonov as a Figure in M.C. Escher's 'Endless Stairs.'*

I call myself "a beautiful man." This has nothing to do with my looks or my soul or my sense of what constitutes beauty. But how can I call myself anything other than by my own name without irony or self-deprecating humour? Here I understand the "beautiful" in Dostoyevsky's sense of the word. I do not seek God, however, but myself. Since I'll never be an old man, alone, and in endless contemplation of the past, I'm leaving these notes for my son, Anton Sergeevich, who will only know that I left him everything, and died young, likely as a suicide. I didn't always feel forsaken by others, rejected by life. Still, I'll be forever young, won't I? I was usually, if not always, bewildered by life. People were strange. My experiences were odd, and if not puzzling and mysterious, often just plain weird. I married young, but loved another. How much has actually changed then with the passage of time and the endless days of struggling to make sense of my so-called life, not in my body, which is in premature ruins, but in my apprehension of the world around me? That world is actually split in two: the younger days (the past) in the east, and the defining moments of my life (waiting to die by my own hand or a secret policeman's bullet) in the west.

I won't begin with my childhood, but with the rebellious years, starting at age 21.

During the 19— Upheaval, I'd tried everything to get it over with. I even tried a suicide pact with a friend of mine, a devoted insurgent, Ilya, a beautiful young man I nicknamed after a Cossack warrior in one of Gogol's tales. Ilya blew himself up in the market, but I couldn't go through with it. He survived, but carried the reminder of it (shrapnel) on his right temple for the rest of his days. I envied his determination to finish what we had started. By wanting to kill himself, he had wanted to destroy the society that he hated, so intent was he on the transformation of life and the new creation that he longed for. Though I had failed to get it done, was it right to be jealous of the heroes, especially such a violent soul as Ilya? It was a jealous life I lived in a jealous city, part of what my friend called a jealous country. "We're so envious of one another," he used to say, "the weak and strong, the rich and poor, the powerful and disinherited, the living and the dead. We live in a jealous state. We even envy other people's jealousy-guarded ideas. And though likely lifeless, they're jealous of us."

When I moved back home, following MY failed revolutionary action, I found myself lost among the members of my family. I refused to climb the never-ending stairs of our ancestral home. It was a vast estate with a view of the distant mountains. I saw that my siblings were climbing the endless stairs in the rain without a word. When they got tired, our father allowed them to turn around and go the other way. He used to say the family was a fantasy. I thought of it as an alternate universe. To accept my place in it, I sat on the stairs of one of the lower levels with my back turned to the pillars of the archway that led to an inner courtyard where it always rained. I had a spectacular view of the southern borders of the recently ravaged coastline. I could see the foothills and the lost horizon.

My brothers and sisters marched up and down the endless stairs. My mother said to me: "Sergei, most of your brothers and sisters believe they live in a house designed by an architect obsessed with stairs." Most of the children did, except for my youngest sister, Anna Antonovna. She told me that the staircases used to be numbered, but then one of my brothers named them: Staircase of the Blessed, Staircase of the Ashamed, Staircase of the Forgotten,

Staircase of the Accuser, Staircase of the Accused, Staircase of the Fallen.

My refusal to take part in the ritual was likely an error, for all was ascending and descending within the high walls of this architectural monster or marvel, depending on your point of view.

Torrential rains battered the monolithic building that towered above all other structures in the devastated region. Some of the buildings had been evacuated and stood vacant. The expressway had collapsed long ago and floodwaters lapped the bulwarks. One of my other brothers stood on a rooftop, one of several, looking up at the stream of siblings that passed before his constant gaze. He leaned his elbows on a low wall and stared blankly at all those who took part in our father's exercise. One was happy, the other, ashamed. One sat, while the other stood. He wanted to be left alone as the only one to stand out from the rest, the one selected to watch. He spoke about setting fire to the place, bringing strife to the rest of the family.

For a few hours each day, we never varied our positions. We remained steadfast and vigilant in our solitary confinements. Our secrecy, our vow, our absurd discipline were symbolized by our unwavering and obedient ascending and descending. I had to admit that there were times when I thought I was taking part in the climb, in spite of my refusal. My father knew how to deal with all our idiosyncrasies. He had given us each a special task befitting our temperaments and talents. I had once overheard him say to my mother,

"They're ballasts holding up this whole structure, those two sons of mine, if the others only knew it. They think they're rebelling, but they're doing exactly what I want them to do."

Were we there to bear witness to our father's vision of family life? This was the question that I asked myself. Yet it went unanswered. I mopped and polished the stairs when my family was sleeping. But I did it for myself, not for them. I liked the way white stone glowed in the moonlight, especially after it rained. Rainwater cascaded in silver and gold. I scrubbed the stairs until my fingers bled and the skin peeled off my knuckles and knees. My father, with his piercing green eyes and hair swept back like a silent film star or a dictator, never chastised me for refusing to walk up and down the stairs. He never punished my brother for his apparent idleness, and how he named and renamed everything he saw going on. Was it our father's method of teaching us the error of our ways? Was this how he wanted to show us the futility of our revolt against the strictness of the rule?

I clasped my hands, rested my elbows on my knees and looked straight ahead. What was I looking at? It was a gigantic, crumbling wall. What was beyond the ruins? A field of wild lupine drifted faraway in blue waves to the foothills. Were my eyes really turned inward, contemplating the sacred duty of my brothers and sisters? I couldn't see them, but only hear them, and my mother's cries, lamenting what she saw. Given my position then, I couldn't comfort her. I had to accept her sobs as part of the routine.

A bell tolled endlessly. The wind was up. I was cold. The only escape from the endless stairs was to refuse to go out there at all and stay inside with my drooping head in my hands. The only escape was to refuse to escape.

I was free. What was I free from? What was I free for? "Free me from this useless freedom," I said, as if talking to my absent lover. "More than meets the eye, a single manifestation of two brothers standing and sitting apart from the rest of the family of equal stature, as nearly as I can tell, and dressed alike in black, hooded sweatshirts, I'm the seated figure ghostly, penitent, ashamed of my freedom."

When would I see an end to this dreadful monotony? (It was inescapable. Yes, even the way I was telling my story needed a way out.)

"Yes, it can be done, despite appearances," I said, as if talking to no one. "The end will cure me of my need to know what was going to happen then. It will cure me of love."

I argued badly then, as I considered the problem of the endless stairs. Merciless sky, above. Rain fell everyday. I felt I was falling. Below me: just stairs. Architectural reasoning, one step up and two steps down, was leading me nowhere. I remembered my father telling me about a man who sent him manuscripts from an asylum. The manuscripts were thick, disordered, and incomprehensible. Although my father burned them, or threw them down the stairs and left the sheets out in the rain, I looked forward to reading what the madman would send him each year until the manuscripts stopped coming, but the rain didn't stop falling. He was the only

*writer I had ever cried over in my life. Maybe, it was the sound of
endless rain falling on never-ending stone steps in a house of stairs.*

*My father said that it was time for me to join the line or leave.
That's right—to end it.*

*"Jump, jump," I thought I heard him say. "Or get in step with
the others, before you are trampled to death."*

*The only stipulation was that I had to take my own life. I did
as I was told.*

Did he? Did he, in fact, ever do as he was told? It was too annoyingly
symbolic to interpret without misgivings about my interpretation. I
hid the document in my suitcase. Still wide-awake, and even more
anxious about everything than before, I considered whether or not the
man claiming to be my papochka had ended his own life. Had he been
provoked? Tricked? Duped? Pushed? Dispatched? How was I supposed
to interpret his life story with all the signs and symbols it contained?
Ilya had believed that he had been assassinated. I was afraid for his
safety. So I begged Mamochka to tell me that Ilya was safely away and
out of all harm's way. She promised me that the secret police (Bagot
and Athol) had escorted Ilya to the border town of his choice. Which
one? She would not say. It was safer that way. It was a form of exile.
But he was unharmed. In fact, the gunshot wound had been tended to
beyond what the Ilya-loving country folk had done for him. He now
limped and walked with a cane, but could begin a new life somewhere
else in the world as an émigré.

If only I could discover where he was, I would find a way, despite
the circumstances, of writing to him, of pleading with him to get in
touch, to figure out how we could be together again. It was beyond
my comprehension, but it was Heavenovsky who suggested a way of
doing what I longed to do. Heavenovsky and Nina were staying in
the summerhouse again. Nina was forced to listen to my mamochka's
endless sermons and lectures on marriage and married love. It was pure
indoctrination. Heavenovsky waited for the *counselling* session, "the
little party," as Mamochka called it, to make his bride biddable, at
least receptive to his touch. For one such session with Mamochka and
Nina (that I learned about later), the "little party" referred to here was
one in which Ilya was derided and assaulted. Nina had taken part in
humiliating him, but she sought me out, penitent, determined to help
me get Ilya away from the house arrest. Heavenovsky, too, had barged

in and insisted that they had gone too far in their mistreatment of my lover and that now it was time to act, to free Ilya, and to help me find a way out of this nightmare. Leave it to the stupidest person in the farce to come up with the cleverest solution. We had to defeat deception and injustice. Our love was the cause. Lovers like us didn't deserve the degradation. He went on until Nina stopped him, demanding a *plan.* I didn't have a plan then, but I knew that Heavenovsky and Nina would be part of one, if I ever came up with an escape plan. The plan would also have to involve an escape route to a new country. And then Heavenovsky approached me with caution and told me that he had a message for me from *guess who*?

"Ilya?"

"When they returned my car, I found a note concealed under the mat. It was cryptic, but I deciphered it."

"You deciphered it? You mean you have invented a message and now claim it comes from Ilya. Is there no end to your calumny?"

"All right, all right, I won't tell you what it says."

"Idiot, or inspired madman, tell me."

It was in the telling that I found out that Ilya had crossed the border into F—. He would move on to Q—. From there, he would make his way to C—. At least, it looked like C—. That would be his base while he figured out what to do next. Heavenovsky then led me out to the gazebo, in fact, the same hole that had once held my lover. (I had preserved the hole *in memoriam.*) He bent down, reached in and pulled out another note.

"What's that? Another of your buried and now exhumed poems?"

"A greeting, sir, from the *fugitive*," he said.

"Give me that."

I looked at the dirty piece of paper, rained on, once buried, but now unearthed and seeing the light of day.

"It says nothing."

"There is a marking on it," he said. "Look closer. It is a symbol. In fact, numbers and a symbol: a location on a map. You must find what the coordinates coordinate to, and there, there you will know exactly where (and here Heavenovsky lowered his conspiratorial voice), he is."

I studied it the way my papochka had taught me to look at numbers and symbols, saw nothing in the markings, but took it inside. I hid it in my jacket pocket. Went to my room. Locked the door and began puzzling out the signs and numbers, if they were signs and numbers at all. I consulted maps. Jogged my memory. Then made my discovery.

It was Heavenovsky that covertly acted as my driver. I wouldn't drive again. Mamochka learned from a hastily scribbled note that I was out and would be back soon. I said I would be back as soon as the road and the travelling and the driving skills of the poet, Heavenovsky, allowed. "Pray for me," I added. "I hate to be driven anywhere, but I must go." I went. That was how I found Ilya where he was: not free, not across a border, but in *detention*, a kind of perverse and cruel house arrest.

"How did you know this note was in the hole?" I asked.

"Well, clearly, I put it there," Heavenovsky said.

"Why?"

"For the sake of concealment and revelation, suspense and intrigue, and to protect you, and for the plot."

"For the plot? What plot? There isn't any. The unities have already been destroyed. It is formless."

"For the sake of the events unfolding, which I desperately want to keep from becoming tragic, even a tragic farce, and to get you outside. For the possibility of starting over, and of overcoming more monsters in your love story than that of your mamochka so that you can live a new life. I can take you to him. I found out where he was sent from listening carefully to your mamochka's ravings about what had happened to him, about the trial, and drawing a line of reasoning to detention for him."

"Where is he?"

"I'll take you there."

"The more I look at this ridiculous note, the more I see that, despite the smudge and dirt, it is not Ilya's handwriting in ciphers or not, but my mamochka's. Is she behind this, too, like the grey, maternal eminence she is?"

"Isn't she behind everything, sir?"

"Where does she want you to take me?"

"For a *drive* at precisely 3 o'clock. Soon now."

"Where to?"

"Not allowed to say, to disclose. A secret, of sorts, for the impact it will have on you when it is revealed."

"Will I be bumped off?"

"No, sir, not bumped off, not if I can help it, and not in this episode, but given a new start, of sorts."

For the possibility of a fresh start, we got into the cheap car.

Heavenovsky struggled to start the engine, did, rammed it into gear, and drove down the long driveway to the road. The first thing that I noticed, besides a few bloodstains, was a black car coming the other way. I turned my head to see it proceed up the driveway to the summerhouse.

"My mamochka? In a Black Maria?"

"Yes. And an important guest, if I can call that type of guest important."

"Drive, drive, you're driving me crazy."

"I always do. But so far not in a car."

We drove through the country, stopped at a country store, bought a few provisions, bread, sausage (for the mysterious *guest*), got back in, and drove off.

"You're going back the way we came."

"Yes, sir, on orders. Enough time has elapsed."

"For what? Further chaos? Mayhem? Torture? Total confusion?"

"For the prisoner to be safely delivered to his community service."

"Ilya?"

"He was tried," Heavenovsky said in love with exposition. "Your mamochka did the rest. He has been spared time in a penal colony and all that means for him, and given a sentence of community service to be served under your mamochka's supervision."

"Say, death, not that. Doing *what* under her?"

"Assisting her in her work."

"Someone hoping to change the laws on marriage is condemned to assist with the rites as written. Cruel punishment, for sure, unusual and cruel."

"But with some freedom to come and go," he said. "You can see him, but cannot be with him."

"I'm sentenced as well," I said, "to be tantalized, but never to have, to enjoy. Cruel. Cruel. Hypocritical, vicious."

"But a new life, sir," he offered. "Life as a protest against prejudice and injustice."

"Life? Life? No wonder my papochka 'fell down' the stairs.' I'll soon jump."

"Or was *pushed*, to hear Ilya tell it."

"Drive, drive."

We drove *back* to the summerhouse where Mamochka greeted me with Ilya standing next to her. In the shadows lurked shady figures whose outlines resembled Bagot and Athol, or the other way around, smirking. Community service with added supervision and enforcement—what the hell, or what a hell.

"A prison for all of us," I said to my mamochka, staring at Ilya who stood with downcast eyes and a little unsteady on his legs. The cane propped him up. "You're a shape-shifter, Mamochka."

"But I'm always the same, Anton. Your mamochka in any other form is still your mamochka."

"Evil to good, yes, but evil to darker malice is still evil, wicked."

"Not too loud," she said. "They can hear you. Bagot is Nicolai Bagotsky and Athol is Anatoli Antunovich."

"How can we live like this," I asked, "cured of love?"

"We'll live, waiting for the ban to be lifted for you with Ilya under my supervision, living as before until then with nothing changed."

"Everything as before? Longing without end? Repression? Suffering?"

"No suffering lasts forever," Heavenovsky suggested, standing close to Nina who joined us out on the lawn.

"Will you be all right," Nina asked, "all things considered?"

"All things considered, we'll always be all right. But what am I going to do?"

I thought I heard someone saying: 'Do something.'

"As ever, you'll do *nothing*," my mamochka said, "but continue to criticize everything. As always, I'll perform marriages with creativity and enthusiasm. I'll protect you, Anton. I'll look out for your man, beyond the punishment he deserves, and the revenge that it affords me for what he and your papochka did to me. He'll get better, improve, be cured, if he keeps taking his meds and he'll realize the error of his ways, his dissident doctrines, and he'll be happy. Won't you?"

Ilya looked up slowly as if coming to.

7ᵗʰ Dose

Curing Ilya

Ilya's humiliation continued at a little party my mamochka threw for herself and Nina: women only, Ilya not included, for reasons that became only clear after his ordeal ended. I had to reconstruct the episode from surveillance footage and Nina's odd confession. It went something like this:

"Women bleed, but the male of the species must be made to," Mamochka said to Nina at her little party. "You'll get along better with men, especially Valentin, by making little cuts and sticking the occasional knife in the back. That's a cure for their assertiveness and folly."

The rule was you had to bleed to be invited to one of my mamochka's little parties. If you didn't, you sometimes got in by invitation, but blindfolded. Males had to stay out until the get-together was over, usually at dawn. The surveillance tape showed what the true aim of her party was: to *cure* Ilya. It was scandalous the way she and her accomplice treated him. As we all later discovered, it was a truth-bearing revelation of the horror connected to her way of doing things. Nina was no better.

"I don't know what the hell the men do when I'm not there," Nina said.

"The men? They fantasize," Mamochka said.

"About what?"

"What we're doing in here, just between ourselves."

"Are they plotting to kill us or each other?" she suggested. "I think Valentin wants to kill everybody. Although he doesn't look like a killer, he certainly knows how to suffocate me, and bore me to death. By the way, is that a surveillance camera?"

"Yes, it's switched on," Mamochka said, "so everybody can see us in real time, and we can watch ourselves later. Everything is being recorded, monitored."

"I'm acting anyway," Nina said.

They were in Mamochka's room for a little party that would give the older woman a chance to "educate" Nina about men and new husbands. It was her night. A little surprise was planned for later on. Ilya was the entertainment. Yes, he was playing the piano, but he was blindfolded, and played slightly off-key. When Mamochka told Nina that she had forced him to play as a kind of punishment, she said it was better than being in prison or being shot. He needed to do something.

She had banished Valentin and me to our rooms, like naughty children.

"Amuse yourselves," she had said, "without us for a while."

I had spoiled things last night by having a fit about the way things had turned out. Was I faking it? The secret police thought so. Mamochka said that I was selfish that way. She had sent Valentin to keep me company so that I'd feel less lonely, less forsaken, but still oppressed, and wouldn't allow Ilya to see me. Yet I saw him on the security footage. It was all for his benefit as a form of shaming and humiliating him.

"If memory serves, especially at my age," Mamochkas said, "I devoted myself entirely to men when I was your age."

"Ilya is listening," Nina was overheard saying.

"Don't worry about Ilya. He knows my past. He had a hand in re-writing it. He can't see us unless he peeks, in which case we'll pluck out his vile jellies. He's here for our pleasure. We're not here for his. Never forget that. All men are, despite their orientation."

"Yes," Nina said, remembering, "Anton's little outburst about injustice cut the evening short. I meant to ask you about his opinions re: everything."

"He's still alive, if anyone's interested, but barely. But his views are dead truths. Anton is no longer young, you see. As far as anyone can tell, it isn't his fault. All of us are getting on, if we're not careful. Your youth is just an illusion. You don't have as much time as you think in your being in and out of love with men like Valentin. The question of our ages crops up a lot. It puts us on edge."

"I blame Valentin for it," Nina said, drinking vodka. "Thanks for having me in, and keeping him out. It's a beautiful room to cry in."

"I've cried in it often," Mamokccka said. "But that is in the past. No more tears now. Let's have fun."

Nina hiccoughed uncontrollably at the mention of fun. As if

she couldn't breathe, or wouldn't, and, as if releasing herself from a chokehold, she broke out with:

"I'm a little drunk on the vodka."

"Already. The night's so young."

"You're not," Nina said, pouring another shot. "Is it still on? The machine I mean."

The surveillance camera was switched off, then on. Mamochka wasn't sure if it was recording or not.

"This is your night," she proclaimed, "a great night to bash men and learn how to live with them and survive the ordeal with knives out."

Mamochka groaned and Nina giggled. Surveillance had that effect on them.

"Quick, now," Mamochka said. "What do you find funny about Valentin and other men?"

"Their sadness," Nina said. "Who do they think they are?"

"Who do you think they are?"

"Little boys in arrested development, the older they get the younger they become."

(She had a minor in Psychology.)

"That's it: never forget they are born immature and deteriorate from there."

"Yes," Nina said. "When they die, they return to the womb."

"You would have to mention that, wouldn't you? That's just like you, Nina. You're hard on Valentin."

Tinkle of glasses.

"He's so young, yet so old."

"Too old," Mamochka asked, "for you?"

"For his own good. He is confused, yet controlling. He is passive, yet aggressive. He is poetic, yet pure prose."

Mamochka was now on her guard. Sipping loudly from her glass, and speaking at the same time, she said,

"You wish to God he had never been born. That is what happens to all of us. We meet them, fall in love or something like love, hate them soon after, and want to kill them before they kill us."

"Out with the old and in with the new."

"Thank you for that, Nina."

"Why did I marry him? Why did we marry the men that hurt us the most?"

"Show off. You know more than you're letting one. You should be shot in the head. Wounded in the mouth."

"A romantic."

"Unsociable from what I hear."

Nina tried to amuse her by making faces.

"Nasty men," she said, grimacing.

"Nasty, but unavoidable," Mamochka added. "How to endure them and prevail in the skirmish is the point. Some call it a bloodbath, a massacre. We all want beautiful men, but where do we find them?"

Nina was wary of Mamochka's approach, especially that night. She didn't like the way she was sidling up to her. It had something to do with what she was trying to do. What was she trying to do?

"Men are untidy," she said, sarcastically, "and they think they're tremendously energetic."

She sighed, musing on the Valentin's energy, or lack thereof.

"If only our men had it, especially Anton and Valentin."

"It's terrible."

"You're referring to their sex drives, I suppose?"

"Yes," Nina said, clarifying.

"They grab without touching."

Mamochka was getting into the swing of it, now.

"Insensitive, you mean?"

"Selfish, self-pleasuring."

"They haven't a clue what we want," Mamochka faltered momentarily.

"You should know," Nina whispered.

"I know. My husband thought he knew, but not with me."

"Just like them," Nina said.

She interrupted Mamochka's cataloguing. She hated lists and labels, she said.

"Spare us the details of your failed marriage at least," she said. "You were once what I am now."

"Does it show?" Mamochka asked.

"Depends where you're looking," Nina said, "and how closely."

Was she being kind or cruel? It was difficult to say. Mamochka munched on a crust-less sandwich and said, "I loved him, don't you see? He was my man."

"Yes, I guess so," Nina said. "My own can pass for one."

"He came from an aristocratic family, but they lost everything during the upheaval."

She uttered murmurs of pity or disgust: hard to say.

"What was it that that decadent French poet said? 'Let's kill the poor.'"

Nina followed closely with her own remark.

"They are unkillable."

Male laughter barged into the room. Mamochka had asked us to keep it down, not to attract attention. The door was flung wide open. We were playing our own games getting along quite well thank you in the room without women. Had we seduced the police agents to play along with us? We knew better than to crash the little party for Nina. If we behaved ourselves, we'd be invited in later for a vodka breakfast. The parties usually ended at dawn.

Laughter lingered in the room. A swirling bouquet, it died out as quickly as it had risen. It had an effect on Nina. But everything did.

"They're talking and sneering," she said. "Abominating us. Their lives are infinite regressions. Valetine's jejune poems express the bottomless depth of his boring soul. He is a parasite not only of poetry but also of love."

She looked frightened. What parasitic protection did she have against men? What if we took it into our immature heads to storm them?

"They talk too much, and finish too quickly," Nina said, interrupting and giving Mamochka little or no choice to contradict her.

"We'll castrate them later," she said. "Ignore them. This is our night. We're talking about survival tips for women. Their laughter is a joke. I can't be sure, but I think Anton is behind this. He thinks he has experienced some kind of resurrection or awakening since his last humiliation, and is now rioting. He thinks he's Lazarus come back from the dead. I told him to stop wearing his shroud in public."

"What did we do before?"

"Before what? Men?"

"Distant dreams," Nina said, hurt by the question. "Our so-called men."

"No, not dreams, Nina. At least, you have Valentin. My husband was never anything like that. For me, it's all just betrayal."

They heard chuckling.

"They're telling jokes," Nina said. "You see how much the men are trying to upset us."

"We have nothing in common," Mamochka said, angrily. "I think of them as a separate species. Damn them."

"Why don't we give up men altogether?" Nina asked.

"They think I'm a tyrant," Mamochka said.

"Why, because you talk and act like a dictator?"

Strange music interrupted them.

"Remember, the pianist (Ilya) has ears, among other attributes. The evening is still young, endlessly looping on the reel to reel or just repeating itself."

Nina was having trouble catching her breath.

"You're just like Valentin," Nina said. "Always counting. Always having his way. What frightens him the most is the way numbers seem to go on forever. 'One plus one,' he says, 'plus one.' Do the math. He ruined our relationship by counting the ways he loves me. Considering the alternative, what else could he do?"

"That music," Mamochka said.

"I can't hear you think," Nina declared.

"Anton's laughter, as well," Mamochka said, "coming from the other room is strange. It's a conspiracy of coded messages between the music and the laughter."

She was beginning to think he was doing it on purpose and undermining her again.

"It's him," Nina said, "Ilya, the pianist."

Mamochka was wondering when they'd finally get to him.

"Isn't he your designated driver, too, now that you have him under your control? Or is he the one who rubs you down and finishes you off? What else does he do with his hands?"

"He plays blindfolded," Mamochka said. "It's not his job."

"I'm sure he gets paid in full."

"Sometimes, with money," Mamochka said. "What are you trying to play, Ilya?"

"Satie, endless and without variation," he said sadly.

"Fills the room with flying bouquets," Nina said. "Like millions of wild blooms, or something by Chagall."

What did it remind Mamochka of? Why, only the rebirth of sudden hostility. The music threatened to overpower them, but then subsided.

"He lacks the feeling," she said. "I don't know what my men see in him. Both."

Annoyed that they'd slipped away from the subject of straightening men out, Nina said, "Very well. What about the getting along with them?"

They gave a little cheer. She had a way of steering them clear of present danger and disaster and getting them back on track. The talk, Nina suggested, reminded her of the sound of rushing wings, and she said so. But it gave her the creeps.

"Nature is to blame. It makes us do what it wants."

"It makes us bleed."

"Someone's been doing her homework."

"That's an important fact, don't you think?"

"Why?"

Mamochka was confused.

"Well, simply this," Nina said, "we're being used."

Mamochka was drifting away. Fading.

"Isn't that just like them to use nature against us?" Nina asked.

"What a vexation," Mamochka exclaimed. "A man, I mean."

She had gone back to the subject of men.

"When you consider how it starts," she said, "and all that bloodshed that follows and blood that flows, it's a wonder we're still alive. Women, I mean. Oh, don't get me wrong. I've broken a few backs in my day."

"To do without them."

Nina, for one, said she found it impossible.

"Well, a man is a man," Mamochka said, "until he stops being one."

"We're simply damned," Nina said. "We try to choose ourselves, but they always intervene."

"There's no denying that little something that makes the difference."

She was talking about sex or a body part. They laughed. Nina giggled uncontrollably. She knew all about sex and its tragedies, despite her young years.

"That little thing that dangles between their legs and does all the thinking for them," she said.

"What did your papochka do to you when you were a little girl?"

"He took me on a tour of the capitol," she said. "We visited all the places and stayed in all the hotels, and also tried to teach me to be a woman. I never told anyone."

"Quick, now. A game."

"What sort of game?"

"Pursuing men."

"A serious pursuit."

"All right, here goes: puberty."

"Enlarging of testicles?"

Nina had hazarded a guess.

"Yes."

"Left hangs lower."

"Than right."

"Yes."

"Spurt."

"Strong and chubby."

"Absolutely."

"Penis grows."

"In length and width.

"That was hard," Mamochka said. "Not as hard *as*."

"Penile pink pearly papules on penis."

"Pimple-like, tiny bumps on tip," Nina said.

"Teaspoonful of semen."

"200 million to 500 million sperm."

"I should have known that one."

She talked a good game, especially about the afterlife.

"Wet dreams."

"Crack in the voice."

Nina guessed correctly. This one hit home.

"You're relentless," she said.

"Sore nipples."

"Not as sore as ours."

"Are boys bisexual?" Nina insisted.

"Maybe they should be."

Would the party ever end? Would it never end again?

"The number of the beast is sex, sex, sex."

She knew her Latin. She had to let Mamochka know and mentioned it.

"What better place to talk about their preferences than here?" Nina postulated.

"We're bound to be kind," Mamochka said.

"Kinder than most," she added.

"True," she said. "There's sexual confusion everywhere these days. I don't envy younger women having to deal with it."

Nina knew she did. She was referring to her own sexual confusion.

"In our so-called men, too."

"Discretion," Nina said. "Someone might be listening with hungry ears. We're on the air, remember."

Nina was referring to that damned surveillance equipment, likely our watching, and possibly Ilya's playing, or his ears.

"Unashamed," Mamochka said, "we profess our admiration for the nude, young, male body."

"We admire it, until we don't," Nina said. "I've never been known to look away. Why, on a beach or at a resort, I've never known to shy away."

She was alluding to her past infidelities. The word she was searching for was lust.

"Or kick it out of bed," Nina said. "Valentin never knew."

"Shall we bring the pianist into the conversation?" Mamochka asked.

Poor, beautiful Ilya, it was his turn.

"Ask him to strip," Nina said. "He had no trouble before. Now he must do it on our terms."

She was giving the orders now.

"A kind of demonstration?" Mamochka asked.

"Let's make an example of him for the sake of theory and proof."

"After all, we've had to strip for them: the men. It's their turn to strip for us."

"Can he show us the sort of male beauty we admire?"

Mamochka remained unconvinced.

"My husband had been all for it. Now my son."

"We'll never know unless we see for ourselves," Nina said, always the doubter. She liked to stick her finger into open wounds.

Mamochka called Ilya over. Music stopped abruptly. Footsteps could be heard. He halted. How had he managed to find his way without seeing? Had he been peeking all along?

"Yes," he said.

They whispered together.

"Remove your clothes," Nina said. "Take off your skin. Strip."

Mamochka immediately caught on. Nina was inspired.

"Don't hesitate," Nina said. "Don't resist."

"Don't blush," Mamochka said.

Was he? He stripped. His belt hit the floor. His pants slid down to his ankles.

"Don't move," Nina said.

"He's moving, blushing," Mamochka said.

"Hesitating," Nina said. "He's teasing us. Why are you teasing us, Ilya? I bet you've been peeking? Have you been peeking?"

Nina faltered.

"I'll say he has."

"If you wish," he said.

"Boots off."

He pulled them off. Dropped them on the floor.

"No, no," Nina said. "We want everything off. It's only fair."

"We always had to take everything off," Mamochka said.

"He's removed his blindfold," Nina said.

"He's watching us watching him," Mamochka said.

"Watch him breathe," Nina said.

His breathing could be seen and heard.

"Entertain us."

"Something I learned as a boy," Ilya said.

"We're listening," Nina said.

He recited a poem that had been written for him years ago about boyhood. Nina and Mamochka slapped him in turns on different parts of his body. One of them left marks on his skin.

"Thank you," Nina said. "Don't forget your clothes."

He gathered his things. Slowly. Then walked off. Slowly.

"The nude male body," Nina said, sighing, "difficult to forget."

"Or forgive," Mamochka said.

"You're trembling," Nina said.

"I'm trembling."

"What remarkable reflexes he has," Nina said.

"Is that what my husband and Anton saw and see?"

"He's moving so slowly that he doesn't appear to be moving at all," Nina said.

She said she loved the kind of beauty that was still, perfectly still.

Evening had become night and night was giving way to day. In the morning, they'd be seeing the ruins again and all their losses. Had they hurt Ilya enough for one night?

"Look. It's almost morning."

Nina was crying. Birdsong in the early morning.

"The morning after an assault?" Nina asked.

"Stop crying, Nina. Anton and Valentin will be coming in soon. Party is over."

She pushed Nina aside and switched off the surveillance camera.

8ᵗʰ Dose

The Cure for Happiness

Days after the so-called party, Mamochka brought Ilya, as if on display, out into the open for all of us to see.

"Are you happy?" she asked her victim.

Only I noticed the trembling of his hand, holding the cane, the tears at the corner of his half-opened eyes. Was he crying? Were his lacrimal glands oozing tears to expunge the illness and cure him of love through purification and clarification? The original quartet had become a septet, but the chorus was silent. Don't talk about it. Best not to talk about it. But when you can't talk, you sometimes cry.

"Is he crying?"

"Insulted, humiliated, as if thrown to the dirt, as I have been grounded," I insisted. "Hurt, vilified, brought to his knees, and how the police agents gave him a good going over after that little 'party' you had with Nina (women only) with Ilya forced to play for you, and the way he was mistreated, and you ask if he is weeping. We should all weep for him."

"Nonsense," my mamochka said, "and if he is weeping, it is with tears of joy for being alive, and being free to wait for his heart's desire."

"For him, the cost for knowing us is great," I said. "The cost to us for knowing him is less so."

"Your so-called love affair is the cause. The cost for him knowing my husband and my son are greater," my mamochka said. "I have already paid the price. It cost me my marriage."

"Why is there *no*?

"No what? Be precise."

"No outrage, moral or otherwise. No condemnation, no outcry against prejudice and injustice, no shock, no defense?"

"Defense as in chess?" she asked. "Or is it a defense of the indefensible, as in your puny sense of justice? In your vagueness, you don't know what you are even asking for."

"Your support, your defense of my dignity, of my rights, and a repudiation of the injury done to my lover. Waste of energy in hurting us, rejecting us, and those like us. Why not accept us, embrace us, and let that acceptance help us to get along? Is it that there is ambivalence towards those whom you consider less human than you, freaks and aberrations, like Ilya and me, and those who are different from you on the sexual front? Why don't you declare yourself? Where do you stand?"

"Stand? Why, right here in my usual spot. That's where I stand."

What could I do? Use words and bad breath to suffocate her to death? What could my words do to someone like her and to the society I lived in and from which I had withdrawn?

This was a standoff. Mamochka and her forces had the upper hand. How could I end it? As I saw it then, it would take 3 bullets to get rid of my enemies. One of them would result in a matricide, and the other 2 would mean the assassination of a couple of dimwits. If I began counting bullets and plotting murders, 3 would become 6 and 6 would become 9 and so on, and where would it all end, including a bullet for myself? Besides, I was a bad shot, and words were my weapons of choice. Ilya and I had made a run for it and had been caught. Mamochka would not let me plead my case. Could I simply plead? Find the right words to beg for mercy, for leniency, clemency? Could she show us mercy? Was she capable of compassion? Could I turn myself into an aggressor, a vicious monster, a human basilisk, say, and betray her with a look or a kiss, a deadly smack on the lips (no more begging)? What if I were to rush her, with arms outstretched like wide wings, clasp her head before she could do with us what she wished? What if I were to kiss Mamochka on the mouth? It would be an acid kiss: to poison her, neutralize her. She wouldn't be able to breathe, kicking, wriggling, and struggling, she wouldn't breathe. Writhing, drowning in a mouthful of poison, her tongue seared by flames, she would not breathe, the woman scorned, the self-righteous avenger, the one-woman fury, the government agent, the jealous, jilted woman, the Mamochka-of-Us-all, she would not breathe, and so metamorphosed, I wouldn't let her come up for air, and it would be as though I were battling with a tarantula and killing it, and since she wouldn't be able to breathe any longer, she would stop breathing. It would be extermination, paralysis; it would be an act of liberation, hope of saving both Ilya and myself from a heartless and compassionless mamochka.

But she wasn't a *monster*. She was human. I simply couldn't overcome the force of her kind of humanity. Why was I demonizing her, not as a mamochka or as a woman, but as an agent of the state, the way others had demonized me? My inverted thoughts had become dark, grotesque, even monstrous: I was losing my own worth as a human being in contemplation of getting rid of perceived enemies by force. I had to think twice before jumping down a flight of stairs as my papochka apparently had. But I wouldn't become like him or them, not for anything. Still, I had to admit that I was responsible for what had happened to Ilya. I was guilty of impatience, arrogance, willfulness, and childishness. I should have been slapping myself across the face for my immaturity and what I had caused. Killing off others was pure fantasy. It was the regret of not being able to use violence to end the standoff. Our history was full of people of action who did not think twice about getting rid of their opponents. I could not seek justice by committing other injustices. Instead of hurting her by means of a fantasy of action, I said:

"You could not have plotted our destruction any better than the way it turned out."

"I did not plot against you," she said. "Rather, you and he plotted against us and got caught: you got yourselves."

"'You got yourselves.' Is that a mamochka's lullaby to put us back in the cradle?"

"No more cradle songs for you, Anton. I refuse to sing you anymore lullabies."

Fat or thin, the lady would not sing. The opera would not end. The glance that went between us was deadly. She would no longer sing me her lullabies. I would have to grow up, mature. She had given me a dose of the medicine to cure me of the sickness of my kind of love. They had delivered Ilya into her 'protective custody' for all that he and my dead papochka had done to her. It was sweet revenge, retribution, and cruel and unusual punishment. The dark maternal force would do the rest for the rest of eternity. For the injury done to her soul in days gone by, where justice has a long memory, and for the injustice done to that dark maternal force with her dark maternal love now avenged.

"How do you know you are right, and that people like you are right?" she demanded. "Our society is based on the family. Enemies of the family are enemies of our way of life. What is your way, son?"

What did she care who we were and what would happen to us in such an upside down state? She would not side with us, but with those perpetrators of harm against me and against anyone of my kind. She had us in her power. Too much irony, or simply not enough for a real twist in the story, we were in thrall to her. Had we let one another down? Had we betrayed each other? I couldn't say if I felt let down. I wouldn't admit that I felt betrayed. But we might have failed each other, like a disappointed married couple. Still, deception and wrongdoing had to be defeated, did they not? They had to be vanquished for the sake of our love. Ilya didn't deserve the degradation. In watching it, did I? I kept hearing a single word with a single syllable buzzing in the mind: *flee*. Yes, flight was the point. We had to escape. That was my sole desire. I had to act, but it was something I could not do. How could I use force against the police agents? How could I knock my own mamochka down in an act of rebellion and protest against her tyranny? Her self-righteousness. Her little party had been a set-up: to punish Ilya, to humiliate him, degrade him, and then to release him so that the police agents could do their worst. Ilya had survived, but just, and he convalesced in a hospital not far from the summerhouse in V. It was that fact and his survival that forced me to look for and find (if not today, sometime tomorrow) a way to act. Maybe, it was a call to action, but if not now, when?

"First Ilya was interred, and now he is interned," I said. "From interment to internment, do they amount to the same thing?"

"Don't confuse the two: better *that* than the other way around," Mamochka said.

From the shadows, as in the unspoken thoughts and what was concealed in our hearts came the refrain: "Let's not talk about it. Best not to talk about it."

"Are you crying, man?" Mamochka asked Ilya with a half-smile.

Silence. He would not answer her. He wouldn't reply for anything in the world. She had to see for herself. Did she have compassion and empathy? Dignity demanded it.

"Anton, is he crying? You know him better than we do."

"No, he's not crying, Mamochka. I am."

"Tears of joy, then: relieved, cured, forgiven."

"Let him show you his wounds," I said. "Let me show you mine."

"I don't want him to show me anything," she said. "You were not wounded. Who hurt you? You're speaking metaphorically of your wounds. What about mine? But we're all happy now."

Heavenovsky suddenly became animated, as if after an enchanted sleep.

"'Forgive our happiness,'" he quoted or misquoted, stepping forward and tripping over his own feet. "Isn't that what Dostoyevsky once said?" He was on the ground, as if waiting for a duck to kick him in the face. Now that he was down, how could he get up in the presence of this company?

"Get up, Heavenovsky, you idiot," Nina ordered, embarrassed by his incompetent attempt at a subversive, slapstick routine.

"Yes, yes, Nina," I said, "Dostoyevsky said something about forgiving our happiness in *The Idiot*. We're living plagiarized lives, for the sake of plagiarizing love and happiness."

"She means the other idiot," Mamochka raged. "Get up, idiot." (Heavenovsky scrambled to his feet.)

Ilya slowly lifted his cane, twirled it until it flipped out of his twirling fingers. Heavenovsky bent down to pick it up, but I was quicker and used my stick to trip him and get there first. I fetched Ilya's fallen cane, slipped a silver ring into the narrow end. Handed him mine, and kept Ilya's. I then stabbed the lawn with the tip of the cane. We had traded canes as though exchanging vows, as if to say: "I plight thee my troth," and the other replying: "I gave thee mine already." Yes, they thought we were mad. But if this was mental illness, what was the cure? Decriminalization? Acceptance? Don't ask and don't tell? No cure for our love. What could I do? The tentative and beautiful answer to the ugly question was to come later.

Ilya steadied himself, stabbed the point into the ground, leaned on the swordstick, and then looked up at me, as if showing me his wounds. Forced to accept what had happened to us and what was still occurring in our world, we must wait, would wait, because, one day, we would be free. One day, Ilya and I would be *free to marry, if we still wanted to*. This was what happened. When I whispered, "Forgive it, *our* happiness, and pass us by," Ilya began to laugh at how grave I sounded, and at the simplicity of Heavenovsky's mind to cite Dostoevsky and then fall down and fall again (tripped up) and still lying there, like a wounded lizard, unable to get up or move, despite Nina's annoyed insistence, at such a time as this, with Mamochka raging, and the Secret Police hiding in the shade, and then I laughed at Ilya's mocking laughter, and it happened that way, jesting at our scars, and we both laughed at the cruel seriousness of our darkly absurd laughter, until we *almost* cried.

9ᵗʰ and (Perhaps) Final Maximum Dose

Love's Booster Shot for Full Immunity

I wanted to leave as soon as I could free myself and liberate my beloved partner from supervised detention. I was thinking of the time when Ilya had been abused, and the time during recovery when he had nearly suffered a mental breakdown, following the psychological assault. It was at that time that he had whispered: "One day, one day, we'll be free." Would we ever be free? I wanted to shout, like a member of the Terrorist Party: "*Izmena, izmena*, betrayal, betrayal." The beautiful or ugly question was: could I do anything about our personal hell?

I had to flee. That was the beautiful answer, tentative as it was, but I had to act first, something I could not do, because I was not used to it. I needed full immunity, not from Ilya, but from the absurdity of what others were prepared to do to us. I needed to act. Action? How could I move others to empathize with my cause? What did it matter to anyone else? How could I use force against the police agents? How could I knock my own mamochka down in an act of rebellion and protest against her tyranny? Her cruelty? Could I take my own life, knowing Ilya was in the world? Could we make a suicide pact and end it all (together), our names joined forever as tragic lovers? Were we star-crossed? Were we capable of seeking the Rabelaisian 'great perhaps'—death, sweet oblivion, or eternal rest? Was it a matter of belief in the afterlife? What did I believe? Suicide? How would I do it? I was not that type of nihilist: no ounce of Kirilov blood ran in my veins. I was not a character in *The Possessed*. Cowardice may be a form of daily death, but it is also a form of daily life. Besides, others want to hurt us. So why should we hurt them or ourselves?

"The cure for love is disbelief in love," I said. "Are you cured yet, Heavenovsky? Do you still believe in love?"

"The jury is still out," he said, "unless I change *love* from a noun to a verb."

"No remedy then, but a realization and a revelation that only in making the change is love real?"

"Yes, and true."

"Perhaps, you're right," I had to admit.

Before I could say or do anything else, Heavenovsky spoke with conviction borne of bravado and insight, as well as his usual stupidity, now virtuous and not harmful:

"Why not come out of your early and premature retirement and use your writing as a weapon, the sword and the pen. And show which is mightier: to bring attention to the injustice."

Leave it to the stupidest person in the room to say the wrong thing at the right time (or the other way around) with all the gorgeous virtues of stupidity to fight against ignorance and prejudice. It reminded me of my prophetic dream when my papochka's ghost had told me to get back to my vocation.

I told him that I did not like didactic stories, that writing for me should impart a shock which was purely on the level of art for its own sake, and who would be interested, anyway, and who would read it, sympathize or empathize with me, and then decide to fight for a cause?

"I would," he said, "and others fighting for your right to love and marry whomever you please, as in many other parts of the world, despite everything, especially gender."

"I feel it," I said, "but will anyone else?"

"That is the problem of all art, and the aesthetic problem for all artists," he said. "As a writer, you must write what you feel and make us feel it, too. Will you write, Anton? Will you?"

What could I say at that moment with the ardour in his voice and the conviction that something had to be done (I was useless with a gun, but the weapon of choice would be a story loaded with *words*, not bullets)? Would a story function as a battering ram to bring down the walls of oppression? Was I capable of writing such a story, mine or someone else's? Could I write a tale depicting the plight of those like me, like Ilya, in a struggle for legal recognition, especially in the matter of same-sex marriage? If I were to write something, would they burn my manuscript? Heavenovsky was waiting for my reply, ready to take down dictation and prepare a first draft and subsequent copies until the fair copy, as if he were my personal secretary, for something as yet unwritten.

"I'll write it," I said. "I'll write my story, if it is necessary."

As soon as I had uttered those words, declared myself, so to speak, and set out a purpose for my writing, I felt responsible for everything that had happened. I was guilty, as it were, of both the bad and the good. I had a guilt load to set down: to be excused and to excuse. I had to love the way that Ilya loved. We had to love alike. So I was not merely a nose, as in a Gogol story, or a mouth, as in my mamochka's portrait of me, or any other body part, but a *beautiful* man, just as my papochka had declared of himself and Ilya. It was a new conception of "the beautiful" as personal responsibility becoming social and political duty.

During my detention or *house arrest*, depending on your point of view, waiting to free Ilya from his confinement and to liberate us from the prejudices that kept us apart, I wrote a story, depicting the plight of marginalized folks in my native country and their struggles for legal recognition. I usually steered clear of didactic tales, but I made an exception in this case. The original title was "*Partiya Pravdy*," "The Truth Party." But I transliterated the original manuscript in an improvised approximation and, in a sense, plagiarized myself with an imaginative borrowing from life. I did it for personal and political reasons as life writing. It was an exaggerated piece of prose, the argument of which was a *reductio ad absurdum* of prejudice and injustice. I set down what had happened, instead of what I had wanted to have happen. Memory was the mirror. Before the authorities could censor or repress my work, and reduce it even further to nothing, a typescript managed to find its way out, thanks to Heavenovsky. Who knew how important he would be in my life story, acting as a dedicated secretary? In so doing, consciously or unconsciously, he helped me to turn my life into a story, and with this simple inversion, deliberately or not, to turn my story into a life. It was a self-referencing tale, plagiarizing myself, to tell my story. In my previous works, prior to my retirement, I had always been coy about revealing myself. I was telling all in a tell-all, stripped naked. Now, I was no longer concealing my identity or my motives, if anyone were interested. I would be as provocatively naked as both

Ilya and Hevaneovsky had been in their protest, but in a completely different sense. Was it a true story? True enough, if a reader believed it were. Published first in German and then in a version in English as a fictionalized autobiography, it was an unrealistic life story in which the narrator tries to tell his tale for the sake of justice and truth. It was also a means of telling myself such a story for the way life should be. So, as a kind of 'call to action,' a form of wishful and curative thinking, for the way I wanted things to turn out, and never wanting to be *cured* of my love for Ilya and of his love for me, I set *this* down, and perversely, ironically, called it "Love's Cure."

Acknowledgements

"Love's Cure" is a sequel to "The Marriage Quartet," a tale that appeared in *The Japanese Waltzing Mouse and Other Tales* (Cranberry Tree Press, 2016).

I wish to thank Louisa Josephine Labriola for her kind help with the work, and her taste for concision and compression.

Cover image is "Love Padlocks on the Butchers' Bridge (Ljubljana)" by Petar Milošević (Wikipedia).

OTHER ANAPHORA LITERARY PRESS TITLES

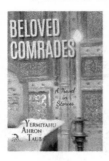

Beloved Combrades
By: Yermiyahu Ahron Taub

Notes for Further Research
By: Molly Kirschner

Falling and Other Stories
By: Ben Stoltzfus

The Visit
By: Michael G. Casey

How to Be Happy
By: C. J. Jos

A Dying Breed
By: Scott Duff

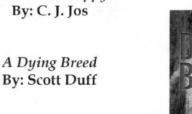

Love in the Cretaceous
By: Howard W. Robertson

Emergence: The Role of Mindfulness in Creativity
By: Rosie Rosenzweig